DANGEROUS THOUGHTS

BY THE AUTHOR OF:

Novels
The Hours Before Dawn
Uncle Paul
Seven Lean Years
The Trouble Makers
The Jealous One
Prisoner's Base
Possession
Appointment With Yesterday
The Long Shadow
The Spider-Orchid
With No Crying
The Parasite Person
Listening in the Dusk

Short Story Collections
Don't Go to Sleep in the Dark
By Horror Haunted
A Lovely Way to Die

DANGEROUS
THOUGHTS

CELIA FREMLIN

PERFECT CRIME

DOUBLEDAY

New York   London   Toronto   Sydney   Auckland

A PERFECT CRIME BOOK
PUBLISHED BY DOUBLEDAY
a division of Bantam Doubleday Dell
Publishing Group, Inc.

DOUBLEDAY is a trademark of Doubleday,
a division of Bantam Doubleday Dell
Publishing Group, Inc.

Library of Congress Cataloging-in-Publication Data
Fremlin, Celia.
   Dangerous thoughts/by Celia Fremlin.—1st ed.
     p.   cm.
   I. Title.
   PR6056.R45D36   1992
   823'.914—dc20   91-22779
                                CIP

To Leslie
whose loving support contributed much
to the writing of this book.

CHAPTER I

"How did you feel," they ask me, "when you first heard that your husband had escaped the terrorists and was on his way home?"

Well, what do they expect us to say? For of course it's not only me: I'm just one more in a long series of wives, mothers, sisters, girlfriends. How many times in recent years have you found yourself staring into the bemused close-up of some woman or other while she attempts to answer this sort of question? How did you feel when you heard he was one of the survivors . . . ? When you heard that he'd been brought out alive . . .? That sort of thing. What *can* the poor woman say, you ask yourself: and sometimes — perhaps a little cattily — you add inside your head: and how come she's managed to get her hair so perfectly set at such a traumatic juncture in her life?

But of course, as a mere viewer, sitting comfortably in front of your set, there's a lot you don't see, and don't know about. The way the camera crew have moved all the furniture around, for example, you'd never have guessed they'd done that, rearranging it all, even the piano, in order — I suppose — to make your very ordinary little front room look more like the kind of room a newsworthy lady like yourself might be expected to inhabit. Or is it, perhaps, not that at all, but merely to make room for the five cameras with their five sets of wires and tripods? Why *five*, one wonders, just for photographing one unremarkable face — but of course one doesn't ask. *You* are not the one to ask the questions on an occasion like this: *your* job is to answer

7

them. So anyway, five cameras, and a corresponding number of photographers and technicians, large, loose-limbed and space-consuming, all crowding in with their bags and their boxes of equipment and wires all over the carpet. There's the sound man too, and the earnest little girl with the notebook; and the bigger girl too — much bigger, actually, quite a hockey-playing type who now and then claps two boards together and says "Oick!" or some such syllable. And then, of course, standing out among all the rest, there is the stunningly handsome young man (well, he's forty, probably, but you know what I mean) in jeans and sweater who seems to be running the show and whose job it is, when the time comes, to ask the silly questions.

Ah yes, the questions: I still don't seem to have answered them, not even the first one; but luckily the sound man seems to have hit some kind of a problem; he's getting the little girl with the notebook to start bleating something into an amplifier for him; so that gives me a few more moments in which to think. What *did* I feel when I first heard etc. etc.?

"Over the moon!" is, I know, the standard response — and of course I should have come out with it at once, soundtrack or no soundtrack. "Over the moon!" or, "It was the most wonderful moment of my life!"

That kind of thing. The way the others all do.

Am I the only one — the only one ever — whose first feeling — and I mean the *very* first feeling, the one that comes instantly and uncensored, taking even one's own self by surprise — was:

"Oh, God, so my little holiday is over! Now the rows are going to start up again!"

Believe me, I didn't want to feel like this. Still less was I going to admit it in front of all those cameras — though, looking back, I think they'd have loved it: something different at last, to set before all those jaded viewers, punch-drunk, by now, with the predictably OK emotions of victims and relatives all over the earth, in every conceivable kind od predicament.

8

It's when you *don't* feel the OK feelings that you find yourself hesitating for a second, hoping desperately that no one will have noticed the hesitation. Because, of course, you can't answer truthfully, it would sound too awful. And the reason it would sound awful is because it *is* awful. I mean, what a way for a wife to feel! How *could* I be wanting Edwin's ordeal to go on for one moment longer than it already had — five days, cooped up, possibly at gun-point, in some awful terrorist hide-out in some awful Middle Eastern slum?

I *didn't* want this. Of course I didn't. The thing that I wanted was peace and quiet; the kind of domestic peace totally incompatible with Edwin's restless and irritable presence, but appallingly, horrifyingly compatible with his continued incarceration thousands of miles away without access to a telephone.

Damn, the soundtrack has recovered! The cameras are at the ready. The two girls, the big breezy one and the small neat one, are poised in readiness to do whatever it is they are supposed to be there for. Everyone is waiting for my lips to open, and sure enough they do.

"Over the moon," I said. "Absolutely over the moon!"

Well, of course I did. You have to lie sometimes. Anyway, what is it actually like over the moon? On the other side of the moon presumably. Bleak, I should think. Bleak and terrifying. So perhaps it wasn't a lie after all.

It's over now, anyway. They are folding up their bits and pieces, tramping back and forth, pushing and pulling and lifting and telling me how marvellous I've been. Pity, they say, that my son isn't back from school yet; they'll be back to interview him later, if that's OK? Yes, that's OK: why not? I can trust Jason to give the sensible OK answers, just as I do. Why, he may even be feeling the OK feelings, for all I know. Has he, on the other hand, been experiencing, secretly and guiltily, exactly the same relief at his father's extended absence that I have? He hasn't said anything of the sort, but then neither have I. I wouldn't be so wicked. Neither of us would.

9

After the TV crew had gone, I fell to wondering about all this; reflecting, rather sadly, on how completely in the dark I was about my son's real feelings. Watching him the previous evening, working so deftly and with such purposeful concentration on a battery-powered Meccano robot, designed partly by himself and partly from a daunting array of diagrams and print-outs, I couldn't help wondering if he, like myself, was revelling in the blessed absence of a contemptuous paternal voice: "Playing with *Meccano!* At *your* age! Really, I'd have thought . . ."

Or something like that. Everything Jason did these days was wrong. If he brought friends to the house, it was, "Do we *have* to have these bloody louts tramping about the place?" If he didn't, it was, "What's the matter with the boy, always moping around on his own? When *I* was his age . . ." And if (the only other option) Jason went out to his friends' homes in the evenings, then he was "treating the house as a hotel".

The things he didn't do irritated his father every bit as much as the things he did. Why wasn't he in the cricket team? Why hadn't he joined a cycling club? Why hadn't he got himself a girlfriend yet; was he abnormal or something? Or — a day or so later — Who was that bloody tart I saw him on the bus with yesterday?

Had it always been like this between the two of them? No, it certainly hadn't. When Jason had been small, they'd got on very well, with Jason asking questions that Edwin knew the answers to, and wanting to be shown how to do things. It was when Jason became able to do things by himself without advice from his father — when he began to seek answers not from his parents but from books, from friends, from the wide world itself — that's when the trouble started. It roughly coincided, too, with the time when Edwin gave up his regular job on the *Daily Winnower*: some sort of row with the editor about the way he had handled some complicated fracas in West Africa — he'd never clearly explained to me exactly what went wrong, but anyway, the outcome was that he'd gone freelance with — to begin with — only very mediocre success. This meant not only anxiety about money — Edwin had always been anxious about money, even when his career was going well — but it meant also that he was now at home for great tracts of the day when formerly he'd have been working. Home for elevenses; home for lunch; home when Jason arrived back from school, boisterous with end-of-afternoon freedom, and often with a gaggle of friends. At which juncture Edwin, having done nothing much all day except yawn and watch television, would suddenly spring purposefully to his typewriter in order (it seemed to me) to be able to complain loudly and bitterly about the impossibility of getting any work done in this madhouse.

Yes, that's when it started: it had improved slightly — but only slightly — as Edwin gradually managed to get more work — particularly, of course, if some assignment took him away for a few days.

So it had been a red-letter day for all of us when he was offered this opportunity of joining a team following up some possible clues about the whereabouts of some hostages who, some weeks previously, had been snatched from their place of work in the vicinity of Beirut, and about whom nothing had been heard since. Edwin had been really excited over it, and so had I — though it had been frustrating that he'd been able to tell me so very little about it.

"It's an out-and-out hush-hush thing, you see, Clare," he'd boasted, his eyes bright and boyish with importance and intrigue, just as they'd been all those years ago, in the early stages of his career, when things were still on the up-and-up for him, or at least hadn't started on the down-and-down. I remembered how I'd once loved that look, in the days before I'd realised how consistently it was a prelude to some sort of disaster or disappointment; to some sort of unfairness; to some touchy git having taken umbrage at some perfectly innocent remark of his.

But one never learns; not really. There is something inside one that defies evidence, and which has, I'll swear, been implanted by evolution for that very purpose; as a vital survival mechanism to keep one going when there is nowhere to go; when all the observable evidence says Stop.

Something like that. How else can I explain how my heart still leaped (though a trifle wearily) in response to this long-suspect look? *This* time it's going to be all right, I found myself thinking, my evidence-defying mechanisms springing into automatic action, so that I found myself responding as if for the first time ever to this doomed euphoria.

"If I bring it off — and I *will* bring it off, I know I will — it'll be the biggest scoop of the season. How long . . . ? As long as it takes, is all I can tell you. I'm sorry, Clare, I'd tell you more if I could, but . . . well . . . there's top-level stuff involved. Just don't ask me about it."

I hadn't asked him about it, actually; I'm not such a fool, but I knew he liked to feel as if I had, so I didn't argue. I didn't argue about *anything*, in fact, during that final day or two — not even the fact that we should have started for the airport a good hour earlier than we did, to allow for the hold-up of traffic. Edwin loved starting late for things, working himself up, cursing the lumbering lines of vehicles ahead, hurling shafts of vindictive will-power at the traffic lights which only resulted (it seemed to me) in making the green one red. He loved the sense of battling through, of getting there by the skin of his teeth — *my* teeth on this occasion, since I was the one driving — and then, once at the airport, he would create a tight cocoon of urgency around him, pushing through queues, grabbing at luggage-trolleys, barking questions at passing airline staff, glaring suspiciously at announcement boards, checking them against his watch, and finally racing and pushing to beat the Last Call to Gate Something-or-other. He loved the feeling of having just made it, of having come off best in a battle with Time itself; of having caught the plane just before it managed to take off without him. A tycoonish, film star kind of a feeling, I suppose.

Of course, these days, more often than not, the ploy was frustrated by the plane being two or three hours late: and difficult though it may be for any of us to get through these frustrating hours, it is even more difficult to *hurry* through them, which is what Edwin was always trying to do.

Can you wonder, then, that I was almost dancing towards the car park after seeing him off? Singing, too, as I wove my way among the snarls of traffic in blessed solitude — singing in my heart, and even aloud occasionally, as the sheer joy of Edwin not being there overcame me. Not there now, and not for days and days to come — a fortnight at least, from the look of things. A whole fortnight of not being nagged and criticised; of being able to do the hoovering without complaints about the bloody noise; of being able to *not* do the hoovering without remarks about crumbs on the carpet and the place looking like a pigsty!

And Jason, too, able to come and go at will, to bring friends in or not bring friends in . . . to invite them to stay for a meal . . . to stay overnight . . . to play records up in his room . . . to laugh loudly at silly jokes on the radio . . . to come out with off-the-cuff opinions about the Common Market or the ozone layer . . .

And me? I was going to have a once-in-a-lifetime holiday from endlessly pouring oil on eternally troubled waters.

What bliss!

That was all I thought, in those first euphoric hours: what bliss!

CHAPTER II

It was hard to believe, but the whole thing had taken little more than a week, from Edwin's departure at the airport to the dramatic news bulletins: first of his capture along with his two companions, then of his release.

It had been a strange week. Where there should have been emotions, there had been phone calls, interviews and news bulletins. Did you know that there are seventy news programmes a day, if you add the radio and all the TV channels together? And on top of this, I seemed to spend a lot of time agreeing bemusedly with well-wishers who kept telling me that it would be all right in the end.

And how right they were. Well, depending on what you mean by 'all right', of course. Anyway, Edwin was now on his way home, safe and sound after his ordeal. He would be here, all being well, some time tomorrow.

One last evening of peace. I tried not to think of it that way, I really did. But what can you do?

Anyway, there could be no harm in treating the occasion as a festive one. We lit candles, we brought in cider, we invited in a couple of Jason's closest friends; and whether what we were celebrating was Dad's miraculous escape, or our last evening of freedom, who could say? Who *need* say?

Anyway, I remember the occasion with peculiar vividness partly because it was such fun, and partly because of the slightly disconcerting phone call that came in the middle of it. It came

14

about nine o'clock, just as the boys were spreading greasy cartons from the Indian takeaway all over the kitchen table, their recently broken voices ricocheting from wall to wall, and setting the very crockery on the dresser ringing. The mounting din was music in my ears; the sheer joy of not having to shut them up was coursing through my veins like wine.

"What?" I shouted into the receiver, "Excuse me, hang on a moment, I must go to the other phone . . ."

And so it was in the relative quiet of the sitting-room that I took the call, well out of hearing of Jason and his friends. Naturally, during the last few hours since the good news broke, we had been getting numerous congratulatory calls, and, picking up the phone, I was assuming that this was another one: but it wasn't. At first, I didn't recognise the voice, and it was several moments before I realised that the person I was talking to was Hank Armour, assistant editor of *International Focus*, the paper destined to be the recipient of Edwin's 'biggest scoop of the season'.

He sounded bothered rather than congratulatory. Had Edwin arrived home yet? Had he phoned me from anywhere? Had I had any further news? No, and no, and no, I had to say. The only news I'd had was the same as he'd presumably had, from radio and television. Still, such as it was, I summarised it as best I could: how Edwin and the two other journalists with him on the trip had been ambushed on a rough desert road and had been taken into captivity by an as yet unnamed group of terrorists, no ransom had been demanded, and the motive for the kidnapping was as yet unclear. Police were examining the abandoned jeep for clues . . .

I could hear the man's boredom and impatience right down the length of the wire. Well, naturally, These bare facts were just as well known to him as to me, and indeed to half the world by now; so I changed tack, and began to ask *him* a few questions. Did *he* know where Edwin was right now? Had he had any sort of report from him yet?

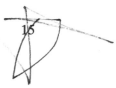

15

"Yes . . . That's the trouble, really, Mrs Wakefield. We *have* had a report . . . he was phoning it from Stuttgart, so he said . . ."

"Why 'so he said'?" I demanded; but the answer was evasive; and something in the man's tone warned me not to press the matter. You see, I am always very careful not ever to say anything that might queer Edwin's pitch — Edwin's pitches so often proving so sadly queerable — and thus, after a few meaningless pleasantries, the conversation was allowed to grind to a halt.

Looking back, I realise that this abortive and unsatisfactory exchange should have left me feeling more uneasy than it did. But at the time my mind was elsewhere. How far away is Stuttgart, I was asking myself? Jolly close, I expect, by air. *Everywhere* is jolly close nowadays. Soon, no one will be able to get away from anyone else at all, ever. Thank God Hotol is still only on the drawing-board, otherwise Edwin might be here within twenty minutes, with the boys still creating this hell of a racket and the smell of the Indian takeaway permeating the entire house. Edwin can't bear takeaways, and he hates them even more when he's not eating them himself than when he is.

"Yes, well, I'll let you know if I hear anything," I said, scribbling down the number that was being dictated to me. "Yes, I'll tell him as soon as he arrives . . . Yes, of course . . . Yes, I'm sure he will . . . Yes, thank you so much . . . Goodbye . . ."

Jason received the news appropriately though slightly off-handedly. "Great." I think was what he said, and his friends echoed the sentiment with hurried politeness — they were all longing to get back to the much more enthralling topic which had been raising such gales of laughter when I came into the kitchen. Anyway, we poured another round of cider, all the mugs were filled to the brim, and soon the decibels were satisfactorily rising again, making a good recovery from my interruption.

There were several more phone calls, of course, as the evening went on, all of them congratulatory.

16

"Yes, isn't it thrilling!" I kept saying, and "Yes, I'm sure he'd love you to ring."

He would, too. Normally, Edwin hates the telephone; he can't see why people should imagine they have the right to interrupt his work — or his cup of tea or his newspaper or whatever — just whenever they choose; but he won't mind being rung up to be told how marvellous he is, of that I feel sure.

It was past midnight when the last call came. Jason and his two friends had gone to bed — they were both staying the night, their last chance to do so for goodness knows how long — and I was wandering around downstairs, vaguely tidying up and putting things to rights. Really I prefer to leave this sort of chore for the morning, but that 'just in case' feeling was upon me, and I knew I wouldn't sleep until the worst of it was coped with.

"Hullo?" I said, a little perfunctorily, I fear; I'd already said it so many times, you see, the 'Yes, isn't it thrilling!' bit. "Hullo, Clare Wakefield speaking . . ."

The voice was strange to me: young, eager, and with a quality of lightness which was instantly endearing.

"Oh, Mrs Wakefield — or may I call you Clare? I feel we know each other *so well* already, though of course we don't, if you see what I mean."

I didn't see, but it seemed best not to interrupt. You know how it is with people who ring up and don't give their names: if you interrupt to ask who they are, they may be mortally offended, having assumed that they were among your nearest and dearest and you would recognise their voices anywhere. However, if you lie low and let them run on, light usually dawns: sooner or later they will mention Uncle Robert, or the mix-up at the tennis-club lunch, and you will know where you are.

"Thank goodness I've got you at last!" the voice continued. "Your line's been engaged the *entire* evening . . . I was getting quite frantic! That is to say, my mother-in-law was . . . still is, actually, she's making wild signs to me (It's *all right*, Mother! I've *got* her! Yes — I told you — it's *her!*) Listen, Clare, I'm sorry to be ringing so late, but like I told you . . . Besides, I guess you're too excited to go to bed anyway, I know I would be. It's marvellous news, isn't it, about your husband? Just super! I'm really thrilled for you. Though actually I've said all along . . . (*Yes*, Mother, *of course* I will! I'm *going* to! That's what I'm ringing her *for*!) Sorry, Clare, but Mother's having kittens; she's just hopping with impatience, and so am I of course, though I've said all along they were going to be all right, Haven't I, Mother? I've felt it in my bones, right from the very beginning."

"Look," I interrupted (I felt I had been waiting for that identifying clue quite long enough), "Look, I'm terribly sorry, but I'm still not quite sure who . . ."

"*Who?* Why, your husband, of course! Your husband Edwin, that's who I'm talking about. Well, obviously! Or . . ." and here for the first time a flicker of uncertainty could be heard in the exuberant voice "Or — I say — you are *the* Clare Wakefield, aren't you? Gosh, I . . ."

To agree that, yes, I am *the* Clare Wakefield sounds a bit conceited, doesn't it; but all the same, it had to be said; and in the same breath (before my interlocutor could draw her hopping-with-impatience mother-in-law into the discussion yet again, to the further obfuscation of the issue) I repeated my question, but this time in point-blank style. "Please," I said, "tell me who you *are*. I'm grateful for all your good wishes, thank you very much, but do tell me your name."

"My *name*?" There was a stunned silence: then, "I'm *Sally*, of course! I took for granted — well, I mean, of course I did — that you've been hearing about *me* on the radio just as much as I've been hearing about *you*. I'm Sally. Sally Barlow, Richard's wife. I've been on TV no end of times since it happened, didn't you see me? I saw *you* this very evening, I thought you looked super, Clare, I really did; so calm and dignified and answering them in such few words . . . And when I think of the way *I* rattle on in front of the cameras, I felt . . . (*Yes*, Mother, *of course* I'm going to ask her, what do you think? But she doesn't even know who I

18

am yet, would you credit it? Well, she does now, I mean, I've just told her, but . . .)"

I left them to it, thankful for a few moments in which to marshal my thoughts. So this was the wife of Richard Barlow, one of Edwin's two colleagues on this ill-fated trip. I ought to have recognised her voice easily — I had heard it often enough, on radio and television, during the past few days — but somehow it hadn't sounded the same. Her face I would certainly have recognised — as indeed would half the world: young, blonde and limitlessly photogenic, the large, lustrous blue eyes being tantalisingly revealed as in a strip-tease whenever she brushed aside her tangle of pale fringe.

And now it was not Sally's voice in my ear any longer, it was the mother-in-law who was interrogating me — Richard Barlow's mother, that is. No doubt in despair of getting her loquacious daughter-in-law to ask the sort of straight questions that would evoke straight answers, she must have snatched the phone from the girl's hand — and I couldn't blame her.

She found it hard to believe that I had not as yet heard anything from Edwin himself.

"Surely," she was saying, "he must have phoned you by now? Yes, I know, I can understand how careful they have to be; but surely, just to say 'Hello' to his own wife! Just a few words so that you can hear his voice! I find it very extraordinary that he hasn't at least . . ."

She was making it sound as if it was *my* fault, and it annoyed me. How could it be my fault if they weren't allowing Edwin to phone — whoever 'they' might be, over there in Stuttgart? I tried not to let the annoyance sound in my voice — after all, the poor woman must be desperately worried about her son, and disappointed, too, that I had been of so little help.

"Yes, well, I'm terribly sorry I can't tell you anything right now," I said. "But the moment I get any more news — anything at all — I'll phone you at once. And of course, as soon as Edwin gets home, we'll . . ."

Well, we'll what? Like everything else in this household, it would depend on what mood Edwin was in. And what mood *would* he be in after his ordeal? Not, I feared, a mood for being cross-questioned by this rather insistent stranger.

"Well — that is — I'll phone you anyway," I temporised. "Just give me your number . . ." By now, weariness was catching up with me, and I had to force myself to realise that the fact that I couldn't lay hands on either a biro or an unbroken pencil wasn't *her* fault, any more than the fact that Edwin hadn't phoned was mine. And so I sounded as amiable as I possibly could while I gouged the number with my thumbnail down the margin of the Arts page of yesterday's *Guardian*.

CHAPTER III

I had a strange dream that night. Well, not particularly strange in
itself, perhaps, but strange in the context of my life at that
particular juncture. In the midst of this turmoil of suspense and
guilty heart-searchings one would have expected anxiety
dreams, nightmares even: dreams of being threatened or
attacked; of missing trains and planes and ferries and losing one's
luggage; that sort of thing. Instead of which, my dream that night
was a dream of such carefree uncomplicated happiness as my
waking self finds it almost impossible to describe. We were
coming down a mountain-side, Edwin and I, tramping and
stumbling through the scree, calling to one another and laughing.
Somewhere in the Lake District I think it must have been, for
though details were lacking, I was vaguely aware of blueness and
distance, and the luminous grey of damp rocks. They do say,
don't they, that if you dream in colour, then the dream has some
special psychological significance; but I don't need any expert or
pop-psychology-monger to tell me that this dream was something special. You see, in my dream I still *loved* Edwin. We had
been hill-walking, as we used to do in those long past days of our
early marriage, and as we slipped and slithered among the loose
stones, Edwin was mocking me, as was his wont, about wearing
plimsolls for such an expedition. "They'll be torn to pieces on the
scree," he used to predict, his own feet smugly encased in heavy
climbing boots. "No, they won't!" I used to retort (and nor were
they); and now, in the dream, I added: "Look, wearing these I

21

can skim over the surface — like this! *You* can't, in those great heavy things!" And sure enough, skim over the surface I did, floating, soaring down the mountain-side, springing like a gazelle from boulder to boulder, with perfect balance, perfect timing, down and down and down. And Edwin, no longer jeering, was watching with amazement, his face alight with admiration and surprise. His arms were outstretched, and as his arms embraced me, I was engulfed by a terrible sadness, an unbearable poignancy: for in that moment I knew that Edwin was going away, he was leaving me. This was our last climb together.

Where was he going? Why? These sort of questions are waking questions; one doesn't ask 'Why?' in dreams; and sure enough, I *was* waking. The mountains were gone, the blueness and the distance, and it was morning. I could hear the boys tramping about, opening doors, leaving them to slam, turning on swirls of water, calling to each other, "Have you got . . . ?" "Where's my . . . ?" the epicentre of the commotion slowly spreading from upstairs to downstairs in an unstoppable tide.

My heart contracted in familiar dread: supposing Edwin walked in right now, in the midst of all this! He might . . . he actually might . . . If he was in Stuttgart seven hours ago, he could easily be here now. Easily! Oh, God, I prayed, let him not have caught the night plane . . . !

I was glad, though, that I'd had that dream, it was a sort of antidote to this unkind prayer. It was a comfort to know that my subconscious was capable of nicer thoughts than I was. Isn't it usually the other way round?

Naturally, the Barlows rang again this morning. True, I'd promised I'd let them know immediately if there was any news, but they weren't taking any chances. After all, how could *they* know how reliable I was? Promising things and then failing to do them might be the story of my life for all they knew.

So anyway, they rang again, quite early — though not, thank goodness, until the boys had left. There is nothing more disconcerting than dealing with a difficult phone call while two visitors stand politely waiting to say 'Thank You for Having Them'.

It was Sally this time, not the mother-in-law. I was glad of this, for I couldn't face being quizzed all over again about Edwin not having telephoned me, and this I felt sure Sally would refrain from doing. Indeed, I felt she was brushing aside almost *too* light-heartedly my regretful pronouncement that no, I hadn't heard anything more, Edwin wasn't back yet, hadn't phoned and so . . ."

"Ah, not to worry!" Sally broke in. "It's going to be all right, I know it is. The fact that they've let your Edwin out means — well, obviously it does — that they're going to let the others out too. It stands to reason."

It was on the tip of my tongue to remind her that — if the reports were correct — Edwin hadn't been *let* out, he had escaped; but I checked myself in time. If Sally was managing to keep her spirits up by blotting out negative data, then why disillusion her? It wasn't as if there was anything she could *do* if she faced the facts squarely. She would just be making herself miserable to no purpose.

"And anyway," she was saying, "that's not actually what I was ringing about. No, the thing is, Clare, I think we ought to meet. You and me. Here we are, both in the same boat kind of thing. You've seen me on television no end of times, and I've seen you. Why don't we get together for a coffee, or something? Or lunch, if you'd rather. Soon, anyway. Like now, I mean? This morning?"

I could almost hear my mind whirring as it sprang to anxiety-stations. Edwin was due home today. They *said* afternoon, but no one seemed actually to know — he might quite easily turn up this morning, and if I simply wasn't there to welcome him — I shuddered to think of the blazing row with which we would then have to celebrate his home-coming.

"I'm sorry, Sally, I simply can't go out today. I *must* stay right here, on the end of the telephone. You do see, don't you?"

"Oh, but . . . ! Look, can't you really . . . ?" She sounded quite dismayed. Then, "Well, look, suppose I were to come to *your* place? I could be there in — let's see — not much over an hour, I should think. The only thing is — I'd have to bring Barnaby with me. Would you mind?"

Barnaby? Barnaby? Not that I needed to know who — or what — this appendage might be in order to know that I *would* mind. If Edwin were to arrive home during the visit, he might just tolerate the intrusion into his homecoming of just one singularly pretty girl; but to expect him to take in his stride a barking, hair-shedding dog or a bored fidgety child . . . Yes, that was it. A child. I remembered now, he had appeared on one of the programmes, leaning fetchingly against his mother — or was he straining away? You couldn't tell, really, so skilfully had he been posed by the photographers, with his mother's arm so firmly around him. Aged about four, I had guessed, and rather Little Lord Fauntleroyish in style, with big blue eyes like his mother's, and a mass of golden curls — the sort of curls that commonly elicit the remark: 'Wasted on a boy!' Or used to. I believe Women's Lib have put a stop to this now, though I can't quite work out on what grounds. Perhaps the phrase just *sounds* sexist, so that you don't need to examine its meaning. A lot of phrases are like this. I remember a speaker once complaining that he'd had an under-deprived childhood, expecting to raise a laugh; instead of which the audience all sighed in automatic sympathy.

"OK then, I'll be setting off straight away," Sally was saying, evidently taking my preoccupied silence as consent. "We'll be with you by half-ten, that's if the traffic's not *too* awful," and she rang off before I had a chance to protest. Not that I would have. After all, the poor girl must actually be terribly anxious in spite of her brave words — or her idiot optimism, whichever way you like to look at it. To talk it all over, however pointlessly, with someone who had been 'in the same boat' as she described it, might be just what she needed. The mother-in-

24

law, it was already clear to me, was an unsatisfactory confidante despite — or perhaps because of — the shared nature of their anxieties.

"What a lovely room!" Sally was saying, pushing aside the light tangle of her fringe just as she had on television. "And what super flowers!" The flowers, gold and bronze chrysanthemums, had in fact been brought by a well-wisher, and I was glad that she had noticed them: they did indeed look lovely in the blue-and-white Chinese vase I had found for them. I was glad, too, that she had noticed how nice the sitting-room was looking. I'd worked hard on it, both last night and this morning, scrubbing and hoovering, clearing the desktop of unanswered and unanswerable mail, polishing the coffee-table and the oak bookshelves, realigning as best I could the books for which there was insufficient space so that fewer of them sprawled horizontally in ungainly piles. I'd been doing all this, of course, in preparation for Edwin's imminent arrival, but all the same it was nice to have it noticed by a stranger. Edwin himself wouldn't notice it, of course, unless I had failed to do it, and naturally I didn't want the house's resemblance or otherwise to a pigsty to be our very first topic of conversation.

"And you get the morning sun, too," Sally enthused. "Sometimes I wish that *our* sitting-room faced south-east like this, but actually the afternoon and evening sun are more important for us. Richard usually gets in about four, you see, and we have tea looking out into the garden through the french windows. He quite often has to go out again afterwards, of course, he works most evenings, but he always tries to be in for teatime. It's our special time, you see, before I have to start putting Barnaby to bed."

Our special time. I was swept by a gust of purest envy; not because she was young and lovely — though she was — but because she actually enjoyed having her husband home with her. They had happy times together, special times that she looked forward to.

25

"So today I'm baking his favourite nut cake," she chattered on. "It needs six eggs, the whites separated from the yolks . . . No, Barnaby, leave that *alone*! Put it *down*!"

While we had been talking, Barnaby had at first been sitting close beside his mother on the sofa, very quiet and good; in other words, very shy. Within the last few minutes, though, confidence had seeped back into his reluctant soul (I well remembered how much small boys hate visiting the houses of their mother's friends), and he had slid off the sofa and begun exploring his new environs.

"I said, put it down!" repeated Sally, trying implausibly to inject a note of sternness into her sweet light voice. "You mustn't touch Mrs Wakefield's things without asking."

Barnaby turned to face us, my brass elephant paper-weight still clutched firmly in his fist.

"T's a toy," he countered, and I could follow the logic of this concisely worded argument. Toys belong by right to children, not to adults, and therefore they can't justly be put into the category of 'Mrs Wakefield's things'.

"It's quite all right," I hastily assured his mother. "Let him play with it. I'm only sorry we haven't any *real* toys for him, but you see my son is fifteen now, and so of course . . ."

"Of course," agreed Sally, not quite listening. "Say 'Thank you' to Mrs Wakefield, Barnaby, and play with it quietly. Don't drop it."

" 'K you" was just audible from the child's lips, pitched in any direction except mine, and then, propelled by his new master, the elephant set off on his journey into the unknown.

"What I really wanted to ask you," Sally was now saying; "when your husband — when Edwin — first told you about this expedition, what exactly did he *say*? Where did he say they were going? What, exactly, were they planning to *do*?"

I'd had plenty of time to ask myself these questions, and I still didn't know the answers. Perhaps, if I'd listened more attentively when Edwin had first mentioned the possibility of this as-

26

signment — but there, how can one know in advance that something is going to go so gravely wrong with a project that one's memory is going to be raked and scoured for tiny clues — for nuances of tone, for inadvertently dropped syllables? All I knew — and so all that I could tell Sally — was that the expedition concerned the gleaning of information about certain (un-named) hostages — information which might — just might — be conducive to their release. He was going out as an investigative journalist in company with two others — Sally's husband Richard and one other, a certain Leonard Coburn. Oh, and that he — Edwin — would be travelling on his own from Heathrow to a destination in the Middle East, and would meet up with the others on arrival. That the whole thing would take 'quite a while'. Also, that he might not be able to write home very often.

Actually he hadn't written at all; but then he often didn't. For Sally it was different. Richard normally wrote to her *every* day when he was away, often twice, and went to heroic lengths to see that his missives got through, even if he found himself up a mountain or tossing in an open boat on some politically sensitive stretch of ocean.

"So you see I *know* I'll hear from him soon," she insisted. "He'll contrive it somehow, I know he will; he always does no matter how difficult the circumstances. I just watch the post every day, I rush out to the postman, and when there isn't anything — why, in a few hours there'll be the *next* post, won't there?

"It upsets his mother rather, that I'm like this: she wants me to be despairing, like her. She was *dreadfully* upset about this cake, you know, this nut cake that's Richard's favourite. Tempting providence, she called it, to make a cake for him when we don't even know if he's still alive.

"But we *do* know, Clare; at least, I mean, *I* know. I just feel *certain* he's all right. Daphne — that's my mother-in-law, she likes me to call her 'Daphne' and not 'Mother', but I don't always

27

remember, she seems a bit old to be called Daphne, if you know what I mean — well, anyway, Daphne seems to think it's actually *wrong* of me to feel so optimistic. But how can it be wrong? And anyway, how can one help one's *feelings* . . . ?"

How indeed? Once again, I was filled with envy. How wonderful it must be to have such *nice* feelings to control instead of grudging, un-loving ones like mine!

All the same, I couldn't help sympathising somewhat with this mother-in-law. In a situation so fraught with danger and with dreadful possibilities — dreadful *probabilities*, indeed, — all this blind, unreasoning optimism must occasionally grate on the nerves terribly.

Blind optimism. Sometimes, I've wondered whether it is really as blind as it seems? I've met people like Sally before — people who, in the face of the direst predicaments — divorce, lost jobs, homelessness — still go around smiling happily in the confidence (quite unfounded) that 'Something will turn up'; that 'It will work out somehow'.

It *looks* idiotic, feckless to the last degree: but is it? The more closely I observe such people — as I was now closely observing Sally — the more certain I am that such unreasoning optimism is not really unreasoning at all, but at a deep and possibly unconscious level is profoundly rational. It's not that 'something will turn up' — it probably won't. Rather it is that the person in question is deeply aware of qualities within themselves which will lift them out of trouble no matter *what* happens. I looked across at Sally, relaxed and lovely against the dark green of the sofa cushions, her young, firm breasts lifting her casual tee-shirt into top-model class, and I saw clearly what her unquenchable optimism consisted of. Warmed through and through by a lifetime of being loved and admired and sought-after, something inside her knew, and knew for certain, that whether her husband came back or didn't come back, whether he died tragically or lived happily ever after, she, Sally, would be OK. She would be loved again, she would be sought-after again; her own capacity for love and happiness was still intact; nothing had happened in her short life to damage it. She was in a no-lose situation, and at some level, conscious or unconscious, she knew it.

And so, perhaps, did her mother-in-law? Was this an extra twist of the knife as she confronted the girl's blithe and unrealistic hopefulness?

I felt I would like to meet this older woman who was facing squarely and alone the realities of her son's dreadful situation. But not yet, not until I had some sort of news to give her. I could see how my apparent inertia, my limp incompetence at extracting information either from Edwin or from some official source, must be just as infuriating to her as her daughter-in-law's idle optimism.

"Tell Daphne — tell your mother-in-law that I'll phone her the *moment* I hear anything," I said to Sally as the two of them left — Barnaby triumphantly retaining possession of a glittering trail of paper-clips which he had painstakingly been linking together, one into another, until it was several feet long, glinting and quivering. I had wondered what he was being so quiet about under the table all that time, and so I think had Sally, but we hadn't wanted to find out in case it was something we would have to stop him doing. Then he'd have been on our hands again, fidgeting, interrupting our conversation.

"But I can't promise when it'll be," I finished, re the putative phone call. "You see, until I can actually *talk* to Edwin . . ."

"Of course, of course," Sally reassured me, climbing behind the wheel of her Mini and leaning over the back of the seat to fasten Barnaby into his safety-straps. "She'll quite understand. And at least I've *tried*, haven't I? I've actually come to *see* you, she can't say I'm not doing *anything*, can she?"

With which slightly disconcerting pronouncement she was off. I turned slowly back indoors, Edwin's imminent arrival weighing heavily on me somewhere right next to my heart, like indigestion.

On top of everything else, there would now be the paper-clips as well. What would Edwin say when he found them all gone, not one left, except for a few maltreated rejects, twisted too grossly to be any use? And below and beyond this lay the more basic, the more frightening question: how would Edwin *be* when he arrived home? What sort of problem would I have on my hands? A man who gets into a jittering state of nerves about a mistreated paper-clip — how would he have stood up to the fearsome and unprecedented ordeals that must have been his lot in the last few days?

That was the most unnerving thing of all; that I hadn't the faintest idea what to expect of our reunion.

CHAPTER IV

In the event, the shock was total. I have just said that I had no idea what to expect, but actually I must have had *some* idea, because I knew immediately that it wasn't *this*.

It was after lunch when the call came. Well, I call it after lunch, but actually I hadn't had any lunch, I just couldn't have faced food. My nerves were too much on edge, and also this was going to be my last chance of not bothering about lunch for goodness knew how long, so it would be a shame not to make the most of it. Anyway, it was early afternoon when the call came, and at first I didn't even realise it was him. There was a lot of background noise, you see, snatches of loud music . . . a strident yap of laughter . . . a high-pitched female voice protesting "But I never *said* he said so, I only said . . ." and then, cutting its way at last through this undergrowth of noise, came Edwin's voice. As I say, for a few seconds I didn't realise it. So excited did he sound, so lit-up with happiness.

Happiness? Edwin?

"I thought you'd have *seen* me, darling," were his first words — and it took me a moment to realise he was addressing *me*, so long was it since he had called me 'darling' — "we were on *live*! You know, *News at Noon*. I was rushed to the studio straight from the airport. I thought you'd have . . . Didn't they . . .?

No, they didn't. Nobody tells me *anything*, I joked. Well, I hope I made it sound like a joke, but actually it was a bit of a sour one, for in truth I was feeling extraordinarily hurt. The feeling

31

was extraordinary because, as I must have made abundantly clear by now, I no longer loved Edwin much at all; so why should I mind that he'd gone off to do a TV programme the moment he set foot in the country, without bothering to ring me first? Why *should* he ring me first, I ask myself? Here I was, dreading his arrival, dreading the impending return to our glum bickering life; what sort of priority does this entitle me to? On the other hand, dammit, I *am* his wife . . .

Still, no sense in embarking on the said bickering right now. Rejoice, rather, that he seems to be in such a good mood, and pray that it will spill over into our home life, at least for this first evening. The fresh salmon, the vine leaves, the mushrooms, the white wine are going to have been a good idea after all. I had bought them with great trepidation, for should everything go wrong and a row develop within minutes of his arrival, then the meal would be a disaster. There is nothing worse than the combination of a quarrel with a celebration meal. I know, because it has happened to us, many times.

So, no reproaches. Nothing to cloud his exuberance during these first hours. All the same, I couldn't quite think what to say.

"Where *are* you?" was the best I could manage. "Are you still at the TV place, or what? Shall I come and . . ."

"No, no, darling," came the hasty response ('darling' again? Who does he think he's talking to?). "I'm not sure, you see . . . no, we're not at the studio any more, we've moved on to . . . (a pause; I could feel his face turned away from the mouthpiece and directed towards the circumambient tumult) "No, well, actually it slips my mind, this chap's name — but anyway, somebody's jumbo-type flat, up at the top of somewhere, all sky and windows — *you* know. Acres of white carpet . . . the whole bit . . ."

By now, I realised he was somewhat drunk, but what matter? He was *happy*, that was the wonderful thing. *Happy!* If only he could stay that way.

It wasn't entirely true, I reflected at this point, that I didn't love him *at all*. It was his bad temper I didn't love, and his nerves, and his sulks and his insomnia; his needling of Jason, his fault-finding, his complaints and criticisms, his boredom, his rest-lessness, his endless fidgety presence, his mooning and moping and rooting for trouble . . .

Well, that's a lot to not love, isn't it? It doesn't leave much. But it leaves something.

" . . . Everybody who *is* anybody!" He was exulting. "They all want to meet me . . . Offers galore . . . One of the nationals . . . a six-part exclusive . . . The producer of *Heroes Today*, as well as the *Back of Beyond* people . . ."

Bemused though I still was, I was beginning to be caught up in his mood, rejoicing with him so far as one could down this sort of phone and in competition with that sort of noise.

"That's wonderful . . . That's great . . ." I vaguely enthused. "But Edwin, I don't know *anything* yet. What *happened*? . . . How did you . . . ? Look, when are you coming home? I'm just longing to hear . . . and so's Jason . . ."

My voice, and his too, seemed to be caught up and whirled away on a Niagara of sound, and finally we were cut off — or else he rang off, I'm not sure which it was — and I was left, receiver still in my hand, and my mind a tumult of conflicting thoughts, among which the salmon steaks loomed large. What time this evening should I start cooking them? Because he might be back, or not be back, absolutely *any* time.

Jason, home from school an hour or so later, took the news in his stride, remarking only that if dinner was to be at God-knows-when, then could he have scrambled eggs or some-thing to be going on with? He had been forewarned, of course, that his father would be home some time today, and had exhibited neither implausible rapture nor unseemly dismay. He had, however, refrained from bringing any friends back from school, and without being asked had set himself to tidy out of sight such objects as might be expected to annoy his father. His collection of boomerangs, for example ("If someone gets hit with one of those things, guess who'll be sued for damages!") and the acupuncture charts which had been adorning his bedroom wall of late (I can't remember what Edwin's objection to these had been, except that it was strongly worded and contained little reference to any of the known data on the subject). And then, of course, there was the Meccano robot, who by now was almost complete and could already — after a fashion — hand round a tray of drinks, provided the glasses were sturdy ones, and only half-full. It could also, with jerky, agonised movements sweep an area of floor not more than two feet across in any direction, though it couldn't, as yet, scoop up the resulting semicircle of dust and fluff and crumbs. Improvements though were on their way, Jason assured me; soon, an area four feet in diameter would be within the thing's compass, which would mean, of course, a double-sized semicircle of residual dirt. No, more than double; something to do with Pi-R squared, wasn't it? Not that it mattered; the creature was to be safely stowed away out of sight this evening, including any controversial calculations appertaining thereto.

CHAPTER V

The next morning I woke with a feeling I hadn't had in years: that of being extraordinarily happy, but unable to remember why. The feeling reminded me of something — childhood, I think. This sort of thing comes much more readily to children because their lack of experience allows them to snatch at happiness wherever it presents itself, regardless of context or consequences. And of course there *is* a lot of happiness about, small nuggets of it lie around all over the place, but adults, on the whole, are scared to pick them up. You don't know where it comes from, they say: you might catch something.

It was very early, long before light, which at this time of year comes a little before six. For several seconds — perhaps as much as half a minute — I simply lay there, revelling in this sensation of unaccustomed, undiagnosed delight. In a minute I was going to remember what it was all about, and as soon as that happened I was also going to become aware — adult that I now was — of all the things that might be going to go wrong with it, whatever it was, and of all the effort it was going to involve, one way or another.

And sure enough, bit by bit it all came back to me — how well, how marvellously well, last evening had gone. Edwin had arrived home in such a state of euphoria as had made nonsense of all my anxious precautions against annoying him on this his first night home. I had been preparing for a bad mood as one might prepare for a hurricane predicted in the weather forecasts — and which then doesn't materialise. Confronted with all the preparations you needn't have made, you feel quite at a loss, as well as relieved.

For in the event, Edwin was absolutely delighted with everything. The salmon — the mushrooms — the asparagus soup — everything was perfect. Nothing was underdone, nothing was overdone; nothing was too hot . . . too cold . . . too spicy or too bland. The crème brûlée, for the first time in our married life, didn't remind him of those other and better crème brûlées he had enjoyed at Cambridge during his student days. The white wine gleamed in our special long-stemmed glasses, the candles danced and glittered in the hero's honour — and how he talked! Goodness knows, there was plenty to talk about, but in the past this had never been any guarantee against the stone-walling with which he was inclined to damp-down eager enquiries: "What do you *mean* why have they cancelled the contract? You seem to assume that anyone who opposes me must have a good reason for it, that's what you're saying, isn't it?"

That sort of thing. But nothing of this kind had marred the relief and triumph of last night's reunion. Our many questions and comments were seized on eagerly, and answered in such vivid detail, and at such enthusiastic length that anyone who didn't know him might have surmised that he was high on drugs.

But I did know him, and I could tell that he was high not on drugs, but on fame. For famous he was, just for the moment. Television appearances yesterday: radio interviews: and more lined up for today . . . his delight in all this was spilling over into his home life, and long might it continue to do so! It was wonderful — amazing and wonderful — to see my husband and son in close and happy communication for once. The light from the candles flickered on the two absorbed and shining faces as they leaned towards one another across the table, eyes sparkling, Jason asking pertinent questions to which Edwin knew the answers — just as it had been, in fact, long long ago when Jason was a toddler. And in the present case, Edwin not only knew all the answers, he was the only man in the world who *could* know them.

So where did you meet up with the other two? . . . Was it before dawn, then? Which of you drove — or did you hire a driver? What happened to him? What was it *like* . . . where the town stopped, I mean, and where the desert began . . . Were there huts and things? . . . Was there any sort of proper road still? Did you have to bring drinking water? What about petrol — they use an awful lot, don't they, jeeps? What did you take with you to eat — did you each bring your own, like a picnic? . . .

Thinking back over the scene, in these early hours of the next morning, I realised it was Jason who had asked most of the questions — the factual questions anyway. As for me, I had been sitting back rejoicing — revelling in the sight of my husband and son not annoying each other, not at cross-purposes, for the first time — it seemed to me — in years and years and years. Of course I was listening too: of course I wanted to hear the whole story in detail, right up to its happy ending: and even more so because it hadn't — so far — been a happy ending for all of them. Edwin's two colleagues, Richard Barlow and Leonard Coburn, were still out there, somewhere, in the clutches of someone or other, perhaps under threat of death. We hadn't, I realised now, asked all that many questions about these two, so absorbed were we in Edwin's own experiences. As soon as possible, I must get him to fill in the gaps, because this morning, as soon as it was a reasonable hour, I must ring up Sally and her mother-in-law and tell them everything I possibly could. Meanwhile, lying there, waiting for the first streaks of the October dawn to penetrate between our not-quite-meeting bedroom curtains, I set myself to go through the story Edwin had regaled us with last night, get it together in my mind in some sort of chronological order so that I'd be able to give the Barlows a reasonably coherent account over the telephone. Of course, as soon as possible they must come over and talk to Edwin themselves. But not today. "Quite impossible!" Edwin had told me — a trifle peremptory for the first time since his triumphal home-coming. "I told you, Clare, I've got to be at Ealing first thing — the car will be here for me before nine. And then there's this press conference . . . and lunch with that agent I was telling you about. And you haven't forgotten, Clare, have you, Channel Whatsit want to come here as soon as possible for some informal shots of you and me and Jason all together — you know, the Family Reunion bit. We've got to find time for that. And then in the evening . . ."

So anyway, it was clearly going to be up to me to report the long-awaited news to Sally and Mrs Barlow, and to reassure them — if I somehow could — about Richard's likely situation. For actually, Edwin's story wasn't very reassuring so far as his colleagues were concerned. Well, at least they were both alive when he last saw them, and uninjured. This much at least I could report to Richard's wife and mother; but of course they were going to want details, as many as I could possibly recall of the journey into the desert; of the preparations for it . . . of the hopes and the fears; what the three of them had talked about as they drove along, "Did they mention *us* at all?" — that sort of thing.

How much of this sort of personal detail had Edwin's narrative actually contained? Closing my eyes against the faint outlines of furniture that were just becoming visible around the room, I set my memory to work.

Where to begin? At the point in the story where Edwin had watched his companions being dragged, bound and blindfolded, into a waiting vehicle? Or at the beginning, where tense with excitement, lit-up with purpose, the three had met silently, in a narrow cobbled street, just before dawn, and embarked on their perilous mission? Perhaps it would be best to start the story just where Edwin had started it.

First, the ride into the desert. No, not expanses of yellow sand, as one tends to imagine; just grey, gravelly sort of stuff, and grey scrub, as far as you could see, all suffused in pearly light from the oncoming dawn.

No, they didn't stop to eat, they had to keep going, they snatched mouthfuls of this and that as they went along, taking turns at the driving wheel. By the time it was Edwin's turn, the sun was well up above the vast curve of the horizon, and blazing cruelly into his eyes, even with his sunglasses on.

"So you were driving pretty much due east, then?" Jason had enquired eagerly. "Due east from Al Bahaar would get you to that settlement where . . ."

"Oh, well, *due* east, I don't know about *due* east . . . I only know the bloody sun was right into my eyeballs . . . you've no idea . . . the blinding rays almost horizontal across the desert, you can't see a thing . . . it's a job to keep on the road at all — not that there *was* much of a road by then, just a sort of track among the scrub. We were doing three-hour stints . . . it must have been just about mid-afternoon when . . ."

And then came the story of the ambush. It was pretty much the same as we'd heard on the news bulletins, except of course that this was an eye-witness account, and not just pieced together from scattered clues after the event. Five . . . six figures suddenly looming out of the glare . . . and then more still, a dozen or so, seeming to dance about in the shimmering heat. Shots fired . . . the jeep tipping and lurching to a halt . . . and then total confusion, a tumult of noise, shouting, dust in clouds all around almost blotting out the sun. Edwin and his two companions had struggled briefly against their assailants, but the odds were overwhelming . . . a dozen or more armed terrorists against three unarmed journalists: in a matter of moments the three were tied up and blindfolded, and bundled into some kind of a vehicle. And then, for what seemed like hours and hours, there was the jolting across rough country, or maybe primitive roads, arriving, after dark, at some sort of small town or village where each of the three were carried separately into different houses. Edwin found himself in an upstairs room lit only by an oil lamp (yes, they'd taken the blindfold off as soon as they got him indoors). The room was almost empty of furniture, the narrow high window was boarded up. Some sort of drug, he thought, must have been added to the odd-tasting stew they brought him, because the next thing he knew it was bright morning, sunlight shining through the cracks in the boarded-up windows, and he was lying — as he must have been lying all night, in deep unbroken sleep, on those bare boards. Someone brought him breakfast — or was it lunch? — and spoke to him, asking questions in a language he did not understand . . . and then, later on, another man repeated the performance . . . and then another. This last one, apparently, did seem to know a little English, for he managed to say: "Tomorrow we question again: tomorrow you answer. Yes, you answer. Tomorrow, they make you answer . . ."

When darkness fell beyond the cracks in the window, the oil lamp was brought in again, and also a bowl of the same strange-tasting soup, but this time he did not eat it. He knew what he was going to do that night, and he would need all his wits about him.

It was a risk, a terrible risk; but the next time one of his guards came into the room to take the supper things away, Edwin jerked round as if in surprise, and managed in this swift movement to knock the oil lamp to the floor, where the flames spread terrifyingly across the oil-soaked wooden boards.

The guard shrieked in terror and rushed downstairs, shouting words that must have meant 'Fire! Fire!', with Edwin close on his heels, and during the ensuing terror and confusion, the rushing in and out with buckets of water, Edwin managed to slip through the outer door and out into the night.

It was at this point, I recalled, that there had occurred a very small hiccup in the new and delightful relationship that had so suddenly sprung up between father and son.

"But Dad," Jason had interposed, "What was it that made the paraffin ignite so easily? I mean, a thin film spread across a whole area of floor . . . It's not as if it was petrol, or . . ."

"Oh, for God's sake, Jason, how do I know what the stuff was? Paraffin? Kerosene? Should I have taken a home chemistry set with me and started to analyse it? I can assure you, boy, that in a situation like that — which God grant you never find yourself in — you don't stop to —!"

"Of course, Dad! I didn't mean . . . I was only thinking . . ." Jason's words stumbled to a halt, and I knew that he was as upset as I was at his father's reversion to this old, censorious mode. The boy hastened to repair the damage.

"So, go on, Dad. You managed to slip out of the door . . . and so then . . .?"

"And so then," resumed Edwin, readily allowing himself to be mollified — for after all, sulking is not compatible with holding the attention of an audience — "So then, well, I made myself scarce, didn't I? I vanished into the dark. It wasn't too difficult, actually, because there was a whole mob by that time, rushing around yelling at each other — hoses and buckets and stuff — as well as half the village gathered round rubber-necking.

"But what *was* difficult was the rest of the night. I felt I couldn't leave without finding out what was happening to Richard and Leo, so I had to hang about as best I could without being seen. Lying low . . . creeping around . . . peeking in through windows, listening if I could hear any English being spoken inside any of the buildings. Luckily, it was a dark night, only the stars, no moon, and so . . ."

"But Dad . . ." Jason was beginning: and then thought better of it. In the last light of the guttering candles I was watching his face, and I could see him thinking better of it.

I was glad. Not that I knew, then, what it was that he'd been about to say, but I knew already that whatever it was, it was better left unsaid.

And so Edwin's happy mood was preserved, and we ended the evening with a celebratory liqueur, served — wonder of wonders! — by Raymond. Did I tell you that Jason's half-built robot was named Raymond? Well, it was, and Edwin had not only remembered this, but had actually *asked* that the creature should be trundled into service to pass round our drinks on this very special evening.

41

CHAPTER VI

Sally and her mother-in-law were watching for me on the steps outside their front door when I arrived. The journey had taken longer than I'd expected, and I'd had some difficulty in parking — quite unnecessarily, I now saw, for a wide sweep of gravel led up to the house, and I could easily have brought the car inside. Indeed, the whole aspect of the place was a good deal grander than I'd expected. The gravel drive curved round an oval of beautifully kept lawn, raked free of leaves and newly-mown, each blade of well-trimmed grass glittering with wetness in the morning light. A wide herbaceous border was brilliant with autumn flowers — dahlias, michaelmas daisies, golden-rod — with tangles of nasturtiums, scarlet and gold, scrambling unstoppably here there and everywhere. Nearer the front door late-flowering roses bloomed in profusion pink and crimson and creamy yellow; their scent floated sweetly towards me as I hurried across the gravel, apologising as I came: for being late, for having failed to bring Edwin with me, for knowing as little as I did — for everything, really, while my two hostesses bore down on me, smiling, polite, holding out hands, effecting introductions; in fact giving the social niceties absolute priority over those matters of life and death which had brought me here.

This is usual, of course; you see it at funerals. Even the police who arrive at the front door with dreadful news are still thanked nicely and offered a cup of tea.

"I'll make some coffee," Sally volunteered as we crossed a

spacious entrance-hall with a polished parquet floor and shaggy off-white rugs; then, pausing in a doorway, she turned back to us. "Drawing-room or library?" she enquired of her mother-in-law. Clearly, the house was going to prove as spacious and elegant as the garden I had already seen.

"Oh — library," answered Mrs Barlow unhesitatingly; and then, turning to me: "It's Richard's room, really, but we use it quite a lot, Sally and I, when he's away. It gets the morning sun, you see. Come — " and she led me into a pleasant book-lined room, comfortably enough furnished, but obviously intensively used as a study. It was dominated by a large, workmanlike desk bearing typewriter, telephone, and an assortment of papers and journals, all neatly stacked and docketed.

I was envious. It looked the way Edwin's study could have looked, if only he'd ever tidied it up, or ever finished anything, or ever thrown anything away. I mean, all those letters he *knew* he was never going to answer; all those journals he *knew* he was never going to read — why keep them? Not to mention the obsolete files spilled out of the filing-cabinet to make way for other, not yet obsolete ones; or the piles of newspapers, each of which contained some controversial article, or some set of statistics relevant to some project or other that Edwin had been engaged on in 1977 . . . Oh, well, it takes all sorts, as the cliché has it. Some men are naturally tidy, while others regard their entire house as one gigantic in-tray. It's just the luck of the draw, which kind you turn out to have married.

I had spoken to Mrs Barlow — Daphne — on the phone already, but this was the first time I had actually met her in the flesh and I found that my initial impression, of a rather intimidating person, was confirmed. Her lined, weather-beaten face was the face of a woman who had coped with a difficult life efficiently and without whingeing, a woman disinclined to stand any nonsense. It crossed my mind to speculate whether nonsense was something she quite often had to stand from her daughter-in-law? It was already clear to me, from our two or three telephone calls, that there was a certain tension between them. Seventy or more I guessed she must be, but she moved briskly and decisively about the room in very white trainers, arranging chairs, drawing up a low table ready for the coffee-tray. She was wearing brown corduroy trousers and a white polo-necked sweater: her whole get-up, in fact, would have been entirely suitable to a teenager, and yet, somehow, she didn't give the impression of 'mutton dressed as lamb'. Perhaps this was due to her still-slim figure and brisk movements — or was it, perhaps, some more generalised feature of our times? I mean, what *does* mutton look like nowadays, or lamb either, come to that? Historically speaking, old ladies have always been characterised by still wearing the garments that were fashionable in their heyday. Thus, in the twenties, long Edwardian skirts marked out the old decisively from the short-skirted young. But what *were* the garments fashionable in the heyday of today's crop of old ladies? WAAF uniform? The Sack look? Hot pants? The mini-skirt? Winkle-pickers? Tee-shirts proclaiming 'I Love Elvis'? The truth is that the fashion people, in the last few decades, seem to have overreached themselves at last, bringing about their own de-struction by changing styles so rapidly that women have simply given up on it.

It was bound to happen, of course, as technological advances made faster and faster changes more and more feasible.

"The nightmare of every fashion designer is that one day women are going to start wearing what they like", lamented one of the top designers of the Thirties; and how prophetic the remark seems to have proved.

White or black? Milk or cream? Sugar? Chocolate digestive biscuits or sponge-fingers? And now, at last: Edwin?

I had, of course, already given them a brief summary over the phone earlier this morning, but naturally it wasn't enough; there were a myriad questions they still wanted to ask . . . all sorts of details that Edwin might still be able to give them. It was a pity, Mrs Barlow senior pointed out, the very greatest pity, that my husband hadn't managed to find the time to come with me this morning.

It *was* a pity, I couldn't agree more.

"It's all these interviews he's got lined-up," I explained. "All these people he's got to see . . ." I heard my voice uncontrollably picking up speed towards that defensive gabble in which wives the world over cover-up for their husbands' misdemeanours. He was quite desolated, I assured them, to find that this visit just couldn't be fitted in, not this morning; there's so much, you see, that he's *got* to deal with right now . . . Just as soon as he has a moment to spare there's nothing he wants more than to . . .

Actually, of course, there were plenty of things he wanted more. Like appearing on the *Mick Dawson Chat Show* . . . like lunching with this new agent fellow who was on the verge of getting the *Today and Tomorrow* people interested: and then there was this party where the producer of *Man of the Week* was likely to be one of the guests . . . Yes, there were an awful lot of things that Edwin wanted to do more than he wanted to drive across London to be cross-questioned by a couple of neurotic women.

That Sally and her mother-in-law were neurotic, Edwin had decided at once, though he had never met them. Whether this judgement was based on things Richard had said about his wife and mother during the trip, or whether (more likely) Edwin's preferred definition of a neurotic woman was a woman who wanted him to do something he didn't want to do, I couldn't be quite sure, but either way it made no difference to my immediate task which was to recount to them in the greatest possible detail every single thing that Edwin had told me about the journey into the desert and its catastrophic denouement. Above all, I wanted to reassure the anxious pair that (so far as Edwin could tell) neither of his companions had been killed or seriously injured in the encounter: the object of the kidnapping would appear to have been the acquiring of hostages, not the slaughter or injury of the victims.

"But hadn't they got any guns with them?" Sally was asking, wide-eyed. "I mean, if Richard had had a gun, I'm sure he'd never have let himself be . . ."

For a moment, I was flummoxed. Edwin hadn't said anything about guns, one way or the other. Would such weapons be part of the normal equipment of investigative journalists in these dangerous parts? Or not? To my relief, I did not need to answer for Mrs Barlow had intervened.

"Sally, dear, that's not a very sensible question, is it? The job of a reporter is to find out facts, to get people talking, not to shoot them." Then, turning to me, she asked abruptly:

"Did Richard have his heart pills with him? That's the thing that worries me most; that he may have been without them all this time."

Heart pills? For a man embarking on this sort of adventure? I swallowed my astonishment and pointed out that this was something Edwin hadn't known about — well, how could he, if Richard didn't tell him?

"And Richard wouldn't," Sally broke in. "You *know* he wouldn't Mother-I-mean-Daphne? He *hated* people knowing about his heart — *particularly* me, actually, and so I pretended not to. Well, sort of pretend, but as a matter of fact I hate it just as much as he does, so we sort of — well, he's careful to take the things when I'm not looking, and I'm careful not to be looking when he takes them. And so it's OK, sort of."

"Sort of," repeated Mrs Barlow drily. "For Sally, anyway . . ." and then, turning to her daughter-in-law: "Sally, dear, isn't it time you went to fetch Barnaby from the playgroup? It's gone quarter-to. I'll be getting on with the lunch meantime. You *will* stay to lunch, won't you?" she added, turning graciously in my direction, "We have a very light lunch normally — " and as I murmured my thanks, combined with fervent assurances that a very light lunch was what I always had too, she added, with a small smile, "All except the pudding, that is. We have proper puddings — syrup sponge it's going to be today in order to bribe

Barnaby to eat his salad. He hates salad; children all do, but he's got to get used to it because that's what they have for school dinners nowadays. And then they wonder why the kids go truanting at lunch time! . . . What is it, dear, can't you find something?" For Sally, dressed now in a very fetching canary-yellow coat and black silk scarf, was back again, and was rooting about the room with an air of anguished urgency.

"The car keys? — here they are, dear, you left them by the telephone." And then, as the front door slammed for a second time behind her daughter in law, Daphne (for such I was now to call her) turned to me with a shrug and a small laugh.

"She's a scatty little thing, isn't she, but we get used to it. Even Barnaby never bothers to cry until the *second* time the door slams behind her; he knows she'll be back within a minute for something she's forgotten. Children are very practical, aren't they? They respond so readily to what *is*, without any sidelong glances at what *ought* to be . . .

"And now, what about a glass of sherry? I'll be with you in a moment, I've just got to check that the sponge is simmering, it mustn't actually boil . . ."

Over the sherry, we talked some more about Richard and his chances of release — or escape, as the case might be; and naturally, on my side, I presented the case in as optimistic a light as I possibly could. Since Edwin had remained unharmed during his captivity, I pointed out, there seemed every hope that the same would be true of the others. Whatever the motive for the capture, the same presumably would apply to all three of them.

"Yes . . . Yes, I know; that's what I've been telling myself ever since I heard the news about your husband. I was very happy for you, naturally, as well as more hopeful about Richard. Much more hopeful. And then I've got Sally, of course, the archetypal little ray of sunshine if ever there was one! As you must have observed, she's *absolutely* certain that Richard will be all right. But then, you see, Sally likes things to be all right. She finds it a bother when things go wrong."

She paused, her large, rather prominent grey eyes staring fixedly into the ruby liquid in the decanter from which she was refilling our glasses. Then, with a tight little smile, she went on:

"She's the perfect little child-bride, is our Sally; and since Richard likes it that way — well, who's complaining? He's a great deal older than she is, you know — more than twenty years, in fact — and I was afraid at first that what with this huge age-gap, and the fact that Sally — well, she's a sweet girl, but she's not an intellectual high-flier exactly, is she? Well, I did wonder if they mightn't find after a while that they really hadn't got anything much in common — no shared interests at all. But as it turns out, they do have a shared interest — that of making sure that nothing ever goes wrong for Sally — "

Here she paused again, perhaps feeling that she had revealed too much to a near-stranger like myself. Then: "My son had a very unhappy first marriage, you know. His first wife was a career woman dead-set against having children. I could see her point of view, of course, she was very talented, and doing extremely well in a large advertising firm; but I could see Richard's too. He longed for a son . . . and also, I suppose, for a cosy little wife to come back to after these sometimes gruelling assignments. And of course, now, that's exactly what he's got. And a lovely little boy into the bargain. He adores them both — absolutely adores them — which of course makes me very happy. If only, though . . ."

But here the confidences were abruptly broken by the slam of the front door and a shrill voice in the hall proclaiming that its owner had drawn the bestest picture of a bunny, much bestester than Paul's bunny, Paul's bunny was blue, "Blue's silly, isn't it, Mummy? Bunnies don't be blue . . ."

The brown bunny having been duly admired — an unconscionably large piece of paper, it seemed to me, had been provided for this diminutive scribble in brown crayon — we all went in to lunch. The meal was set out on a blue-and-white checked cloth in a large, stunningly clean kitchen, shining with labour-saving appliances. Well, our kitchen is full of labour-

48

saving appliances too, but it is many a long day since they either shone or saved any labour. You see, when Edwin is in one of his good moods he is liable to go off on a saving-spree, spotting bargains in second-hand shops and on the local newsagents' notice boards; and that same afternoon along comes some enormous thing, carried by two sturdy chaps as well as Edwin, and only after it is installed on its squat, chipped feet, its rusty hinges groaning, does it become clear that the wiring contravenes today's safety standards, or that an essential spare part is missing and no longer obtainable, or that the whole thing is four inches wider than the alcove that Edwin had had in mind for it.

You may well ask — as do some of my more liberated friends — why I didn't occasionally turn on him, yelling "Get that bloody thing out of my kitchen!" But you have to remember that in our house, Edwin's good moods are like gold-dust, and not to be shattered by so inhospitable a reception of his newly acquired treasures.

And anyway, one does learn to live with them, and they do provide extra surfaces. Last year's Christmas cards, for instance, still repose, unsorted, in the bowl of the thing that is supposed to churn milk and unsalted butter into cream; and on top of the microwave with the faulty wiring I keep the saucepans that are too burnt to use any more, but not quite burnt enough to be thrown away.

A place for everything and everything in its place, as our grandmothers used to say.

We were more than half way through the meal — the syrup sponge had just been set down in all its steaming golden glory — when Sally suddenly burst out:

"Oh! That reminds me!" (Though how a syrup sponge could remind her of any such thing I never did discover.) "The Leonard woman rang up. She had an urgent question and wanted us to ring her before twelve while Clare was still here. But of course Clare *is* still here, and so . . . Well, anyway, I'm sorry—I should have told you before."

49

Yes, you bloody well should, I thought, and glancing at Daphne's face I could see her thinking exactly the same thing, with pursed lips.

The Leonard woman. That would be Leonard Coburn's wife Jessica, of course. This was the first time, to my knowledge, that she had made any attempt to contact either me or Sally: and when I had tried to contact her I had had no success. The phone just rang and rang in the Coburns' windswept stone farmhouse on the Norfolk coast, and I had come to the conclusion that she must be away — staying with relatives, perhaps, to give her support through this anxious time. Now, it flashed across my mind that perhaps she, alone among us three wives, had actually got herself over to Beirut in order to — well, I don't know, what *could* one do? — but all the same, Brownie points to her for trying. And perhaps she had indeed learned something?

If so, we were destined not to hear it that day. Once again, the phone just rang and rang in the deserted house. We must already have left it too late, and Sally, whose fault it was, said once again that she was sorry, ever so sorry, but after all, we could try again later, couldn't we? On which unsatisfactory note we returned disconsolately to our cooling golden pudding.

CHAPTER VII

I arrived home at something after four, and found Edwin already there. Not in the flesh, you understand, but on the box, happy and mouthing. For several moments I did not turn the sound on, such a joy was it to see him in such a good mood, uncomplicated by what he might be saying.

But no sooner was the sound on, than I became aware that all was not going entirely well. The interviewer was out to get him. I'd seen this technique before — maybe it was the same interviewer? Very like him anyway — a middle-aged sort of young man, not fat exactly, but somehow bloated with well-being and upward-mobility. They tend to set up this kind of interview when someone — in the opinion of someone else — has been getting too good a run for his money and needs taking down a peg. I trembled for my poor Edwin. He wasn't up to it, I felt sure. Apart from these last two or three hectic days, he hadn't had any experience of appearing on TV and no skill at all — it was already evident — in parrying loaded questions. Did he realise that this smooth-tongued professional was even now moving in for the kill?

"So you just went off and left your companions to their fate — is that what you're saying?" His interrogator was asking, his gimlet eyes under their sleepy lids watching for Edwin to get rattled.

Which he did, of course, poor Edwin.

"Oh — I say . . . ! No, I mean, look here, it wasn't like that!"

51

"Not like what?" His tormentor was smiling now, an easy victor. "You mean you *didn't* leave them? But you told us just a moment ago that . . ."

"Yes, yes, of course I — Well, I mean, there was nothing else I could do. I did try to — well, like I told you . . . but I didn't know where they . . . and soon it would begin to get light. I'd have been recaptured instantly if . . ."

"Yes, yes, of course, we all understand. I expect I'd have done the same myself; I don't pretend to be a hero. Relax, Eddie!" (Yes, he was 'Eddie' by now to all the world except for his family and friends.) "Just relax, calm down, nobody's blaming you, not for one minute. We just want to get the sequence straight, OK? You were scared of being recaptured, and so off you went. On your own. While it was still dark. Right? That would be the Tuesday, I take it?"

I saw Edwin give a tiny start. *Tuesday*? he was thinking; and then he nodded.

"Yes, Tuesday."

"So, OK, you walked across the desert all through Tuesday and into the next night — Wednesday night. Right? How was it Eddie, alone in the desert at night? How did you feel?"

Edwin had recovered himself. You could see him feeling that he had successfully hauled himself back on to firm ground; and now here he was, describing to millions of viewers the scene that he had described to Jason and me, using almost the same words, waxing eloquent about the velvet blackness of the sky, the brilliance of the stars.

Casually, the interviewer glanced down at some kind of document that happened to be conveniently to hand.

"It seems it was full moon on that Tuesday night," he drawled. "Funny the sky was so black and the stars so brilliant. You'd have thought . . ."

Now what? Oh, poor Edwin . . . !

For a moment he just stared, his mouth opening and shutting soundlessly. Then:

52

"You forget, I was two thousand miles east of here," he countered. "It may have been full moon here in England, but where I was . . ."

I covered my face with my hands, not wanting to witness the humiliation that would follow on this idiot remark. Poor Edwin! Poor, baffled Edwin . . .!

But when I cautiously uncovered my eyes and ventured to glance again at the screen, I saw, to my amazement that it was the interviewer, not Edwin, who was floundering. I watched this highly paid professional, glossy with success, frantically trying to work out whether the moon is, or is not, at the same phase in every part of the world. One had to feel sorry for the man. After all, it must be many a long year since teacher had explained about tides, and the phases of the moon, patiently tapping and prodding at the wall-charts with her long stick. And naturally, once out of primary school, he had never had occasion to think about the moon ever again, or even look at it, why should he? After all, he wasn't on the *Sky at Night* team, was he, he was on Current Affairs, for God's sake! In fact, the whole thing was a bit below the belt — it was as if Edwin had committed a foul and got away with it.

Good old Edwin! So I would be siding with a winner, after all!

Siding? Taking sides? About what? Against whom?

It's strange the way unwelcome suspicions can float unacknowledged around one's skull, like a boatload of refugees, unwanted, not allowed to land anywhere, yet all the time becoming more insistent, more inescapable. Thus it is that when the moment of revelation comes it isn't a shock at all, because by then you realise that you've known it all along.

Not that this *was* the final revelation, this about the full moon; it was just one more thing on top of all the other small discrepancies in Edwin's account of his adventures; the gaps in it, the bits that didn't quite add up; not least of which was Edwin's glowing and buoyant good health at the end of his ordeal. The beating-up; the two days of incarceration and interrogation; the powerful dose of some mysterious drug; the hair-raising escape; the forty-mile trek across empty desert without so much as a bottle of water to sustain him: would one not expect a man to arrive home in a somewhat battered and exhausted state after all this?

A man like Edwin, I mean. Of course, I know there are people who will swim across twenty miles of shark-infested water and then step ashore bronzed and smiling, declaring there was nothing to it, anyone could have done it.

But not Edwin, I assure you. There are so many things, you see, that Edwin can't stand, and I am quite certain that swimming across twenty miles of shark-infested water would be one of them, together with fixing a new typewriter ribbon, moving his papers out of the way of the window cleaner, and finding cold used tea-bags at the bottom of the teapot. He just isn't the stiff-upper-lip type; never has been.

But wait; perhaps I am wrong? Suppose they were to come with their cameras and sound-track stuff and *televise* him fixing the typewriter ribbon and coping with the used tea-bags — would the scenario then not be entirely changed? Would he not then perform these chores willingly, joyfully, over and over again if necessary, until he got it right? ("A little further to left, please Eddie, we want to get the light on the hand that's holding the teapot".) In the same way it could be that under the stimulus of fame, under the bright lights of television, his reaction to the hardships and dangers he had undergone might . . .

It was at this point in my speculations that the telephone rang, and as soon as I learned who it was, I hastened to switch off the TV. This was going to need concentration.

Concentration, and tact as well, because I guessed at once what my caller was going to ask, and also that Edwin wasn't going to like it, not one little bit; but I could hardly tell her this outright.

For this was Jessica Coburn, the third member of the Club — the Club consisting of us wives, I mean; randomly selected women linked willy-nilly and irrevocably by the fact that our

54

husbands had planned together this ill-fated journey into God-knows-where. So far, this Mrs Coburn and I had never met; we had experienced only an uneasy crossed-wire sort of relationship, consisting of missed telephone calls and the occasional sight of one another mouthing sweet this-that-and-the-others on the TV screen.

"Ah, Jessica!" I began (well, we were obviously going to be pitched headlong into Christian name terms in almost no time at all, so why not start that way?). "I'm so glad we've made contact at last, I did try to ring you from Sally's but . . ."

"From Mrs Barlow's," she corrected me lightly. "Yes, I'm afraid you left it rather late, Mrs Wakefield, I'd had to go out. I stayed in as long as I could waiting for your call, but I was due at the doctor's at four-fifteen, and so . . ."

Already, in less than forty seconds, she had given me a lot to make amends for. For the uncalled-for intimacy of calling her 'Jessica' when she was still calling me 'Mrs Wakefield'; for having failed to telephone at the time requested; and now for having made her late at the doctor's with who knew what dire results?

This last was the most difficult. It's always awkward when people tell you they've been to the doctor, or to a hospital appointment, without telling you why. You have to say *something* vaguely sympathetic, but the vaguely sympathetic remark appropriate to a prescription for cough-mixture is very different from the sympathetic remark appropriate to a diagnosis of inoperable cancer; and any probing for clues on your part simply sounds like impertinent curiosity.

"I'm so sorry," I began, trying to make the words sound both as heartfelt and as non-specific as I possibly could, but fortunately Jessica (as I shall persist in calling her) broke in:

"You've no idea how *difficult* it all is," she was complaining. "I suppose in London it's all right, you can find a chemist open at any hour of the night, but here, we're only a tiny village, you know. If you don't get your prescription in by five-thirty, you've had it. Another night without sleep — I don't know how I'll be able to stand it. Worrying and worrying . . . Listening to the waves breaking, all night long. We're right on the coast, you know, in a direct line to the North Pole . . . You lie there, hour after hour; the house creaks, and you think of the erosion, the land being eaten away and eaten away . . . The coast line is being eroded, you know, year by year, I daresay you've read about it . . . It's Norfolk I'm talking about, the north coast of Norfolk . . . You did know, did you, that we live in Norfolk . . .?"

Well, I did, yes: it had been quite a business looking up the number in the Directory as it was one of those villages where if the number has more than five digits you have to do this, whereas if it has seven or less you have to do that. Jessica's number, needless to say, had six: the long-term result of which was that you were switched on to a golden girl who kept crooning: "This number has now been discontinued, please consult King's Lynn 50574; which, when consulted, gave you a second golden girl directing you to the number you had first looked up. You could go round and round the cycle as often as you pleased, it was up to you. None of the golden voices ever got tired of it, they were bound to win in the end.

Still, this was no time to be discussing the shortcomings of telephonic communication: Jessica Coburn was ringing about something important. 'An urgent question,' Sally had said, and I braced myself to answer it. I say 'braced' because it was clearly going to involve Edwin, and he wasn't here to answer for himself. Mind you, I knew very well it would have been a lot worse if he had been, but all the same it was going to be difficult.

"So you see," Jessica Coburn was concluding, "I *must* see your husband. He was the last person to see and talk to Leonard, and I just have to know — well — the details. All he can remember of what my husband said . . . how he was feeling. How he — well, you know, all the obvious things. Were they *expecting* that something like this might happen? I mean, let's face it, they must have talked about *something* during a seven-hour drive, and in all his TV appearances your husband hasn't said one word about this . . . or about how the other two were feeling . . . Nothing!"

Automatically, as wives do, I tried to defend Edwin. The pressure he was under; the nervous strain. The artificiality of TV interviews, the amount they cut out of them before they go on the air: and then Edwin still being in a state of shock after his ordeal . . .

He wasn't, of course; never had I known him in such good form, so pleased with himself, but of course these were not the OK things to say. By now, I knew quite well what *were* the OK things, and I said them. After a few days — or even a few hours — of media attention you find your tongue saying the right things quite automatically, without any thought or effort, the way your fingers find the right keys on a typewriter.

"Yes, yes, of course I understand," Jessica was saying impatiently (meaning that she didn't, and that in her view Edwin's account of the disaster had been grossly inadequate). "That's why it's so important that I should *see* him . . . have a proper talk. Naturally, I'm not going to expect him to drive all the way up here — I'm sure he's far too busy (a euphemism, I'm sure, for 'far too selfish'). So perhaps it will be best if I come to you. As soon as possible, if you don't mind. How about tomorrow? I'm afraid I'll have to come by train. I can't drive because I'm on these tranquilizers, and my doctor says . . . Listen, there's a train getting into Liverpool Street just after twelve, and I could . . ."

Lunch, that meant. As well as going to Liverpool Street to meet her. And I suppose, looking on the black side, I ought to ask her to stay the night, really, coming all that way . . .

How much of this programme would I be able to sell to Edwin? It would depend, presumably, on how many name-dropping parties and glitzy chat shows he'd got lined-up for tomorrow.

No, it mustn't depend on that. He'd *got* to see this woman. It was cruel to leave these other wives in an agony of uncertainty, tormented by unanswered questions. This was something he had *got* to do.

"Lunch, then," I heard myself saying. "—We'll be looking forward to it very much" — and after a short exchange about meeting her at the entrance to the platform, and about her not being able to eat anything with cheese in it because of her anti-depressants, we rang off, and I settled down, as Napoleon might, or Alexander the Great, to plan in every detail my campaign for getting Edwin to behave properly when the time came.

I felt weary already. They talk about wives who allow themselves to be doormats, but actually it's more like being a whole carpet under which your husband's social gaffes have to be swept.

CHAPTER VIII

Jessica Coburn looked slightly older than she had on television — well, I suppose we all did — and also more fragile. Her very fine white skin had an appearance of being stretched taut across the delicate bone-structure beneath — as, indeed, it may have been, so tightly dragged back was her black, glistening hair. It was fastened at the back into a lithe, lustrous pony-tail, gripped into position by a large silver buckle.

Lunch was nearly over, and Edwin (savagely coached by me in the privacy of the kitchen) was behaving reasonably well, considering that he was being expected to spend two precious hours on the concerns of someone other than himself. Mind you, I think the jet-black pony-tail had something to do with it — not one thread of grey, though she was certainly at least forty. She gave the impression of being someone who might be in films, or a writer, or something: the sort of person you would be rude to at your peril. He was playing for safety, I could see, until it became clear that she couldn't (or perhaps could?) get him anywhere.

Besides, he had me to prompt him, and to make little hostessy noises to deflect any questions which seemed about to irritate him. Like the scorpions. No, there weren't any scorpions; why would there be? Well, Leonard (yes, we were on Christian names at last) — had travelled in that part of the country many times. He'd been on a *Wild Life of the Desert* team not too long ago, and they'd got some wonderful shots of scorpions mating. I'm surprised he never mentioned it, going right past the very . . .

59

Edwin's voice was becoming edgy.

"Yes, well, we were on a slightly more important mission this time than spying on creepy-crawlies. We didn't have much attention to spare for . . ."

So what *did* they pay attention to? Cooped up for seven or eight hours in a jeep, they must have talked about *something*. Didn't he even tell you . . . ?

Little hostess-laugh from me, in the nick of time:

"My dear, you know what men are! I don't want to be sexist, but let's face it, if it had been three *women* driving along together for all those hours, they'd have exchanged their entire life stories, down to the last detail. They'd have covered absentee fathers, morning sickness, driving tests, epidurals and the scripture teacher who frightened them about Hell. But men aren't like that, they really aren't. I can quite imagine them driving along for a whole day and speaking about nothing but the road surface and the vehicle's oil consumption . . ."

I don't know if Edwin was duly grateful for this inspired intervention, but it did give him time to think, or to jog his memory, or whatever.

"Yes, well, actually Leo *did* mention the wild life bit, now I come to think of it. He did point out one or two — Oh, lizards and things amongst the scrub as we went past. Little yellow things, basking in the sunshine."

"*Basking* . . .? With a great noisy jeep crashing past? But it's only if you stay very quiet, and don't move, that you have any chance at all of . . ."

Again the edginess. "Yes, well, we *were* being quiet at just that moment, as it happens. We were just sitting. Resting, you know. You couldn't just keep going and going in that sort of heat with no rest at all. People don't realise . . ."

Accusatory he was beginning to sound, and aggrieved, too, that he should be expected to have endured such a journey without any rest breaks at all.

And so the afternoon went on. It was plain that Jessica was left dissatisfied with Edwin's account of the journey, just as the Barlows had been, and I tried to fill in the yawning, desert-dry gaps with little flutters of inconsequential optimism worthy of Sally herself ("I'm *sure* he'll be all right. We've been lucky, I know, Edwin being the one to get home first, but I feel certain the others . . ."). And so on and so on.

At last the afternoon drew to its unsatisfactory close, with Edwin more and more ungracious by the minute, looking at his watch more and more ostentatiously. Clearly, he had decided by now that the lady was not, after all, in films or journalism or anything else that could push him another rung up the ladder of fame, or even get him invited to another trendy party. He had forgotten, of course (if he had ever taken it in) that his colleague Leonard Coburn lived in a remote village on the north coast of Norfolk, a region in which trendy parties were likely to be thin on the ground.

By the time our visitor had left, Jason had arrived home from school, and one way and another I had no chance of talking to Edwin on his own. I'm not sure what I wanted to say to him, but certainly something, if only about those inhospitable glances at his watch. I wasn't sure where to begin. Bringing your husband to book about the way he behaves to visitors is one of the trickiest areas in the whole of marriage, and there is nothing in the marriage service to give guidance: to all thy social gaffes I will turn a blind eye — something like that? Or will cover-up for thee? Or will ring up those whom thou hast offended and assure them that thou didst not mean that at all, thou didst mean something quite different, but didst express it badly?

Or, of course, resort to a stand-up row, ending with, "If only your friends weren't all so bloody boring, I wouldn't *need* to go to sleep while they're talking".

Not that it came to that on this occasion. What with Jason being around, and what with the constant telephone calls which had become the background to our lives of late, we did not really meet up again until it was time for the six o'clock news, for which occasion the three of us gathered round the set, tense with expectation. Well, I was tense, anyway, for at any moment some sort of news might be released concerning the fate of Leonard and Richard. Already I was much exercised in my mind about what exactly I would do if and when the news came through that they were dead — as, alas, was all too likely. Despite the reassuring noises I naturally made when talking to the missing men's anxious womenfolk, I knew in my heart that a happy outcome was extremely unlikely. Few terrorist victims in that part of the world ever lived to tell the tale, and it was obvious that with every passing day the likelihood that the two were still alive grew less. If the motive for their capture had been ransom, or the release of imprisoned terrorists somewhere in the world, then the demand would surely have been made by now?

Edwin must know this too. His body-language as he sat, hunched forward towards the set, lips tightly clenched, knuckles white, told me that he was at least as anxious as I was. More so, presumably, for he knew these men personally; they were his colleagues.

Oh, what relief! How marvellous — how incredibly marvellous! They had been released, both of them, and were on the way home! Well, not quite that, for apparently Leonard Coburn was in hospital out there with concussion and broken ribs — but goodness, all the same, how marvellous! I could feel my face, my whole body lit up with relief and excitement as I turned to share the moment with Edwin.

Share it? But what was this? What was happening to Edwin . . .? *What the hell* was happening . . . Cowering back into his chair, glaring into the set like a creature at bay . . . face contorted with — what? Terror? Rage? The sight of him stopped me in my tracks. "How wonderful!" I'd been about to say — or something of the sort — but the words froze on my lips. Yes, they really did, I could feel the icy chill constricting my very jaw.

Had Jason noticed his father's behaviour? Or mine, come to

that? Out of the corner of my eye — for I dared not make eye-to-eye contact with the boy for fear of what wordless message might flash between us — I tried to gauge his thoughts, but it was impossible. His attention seemed still to be focused entirely on the TV screen, which by now was occupied by a caring and puckered face expounding some caring and unshakeable opinion about the New Maths, was it, or fashion for the under-fives? Anyway, Jason wasn't looking at either me or his father — maybe hadn't given either of us a glance throughout the programme. His face betrayed neither shock nor elation, but of course that proved nothing because mine didn't either. I had got it under control without even trying; I could feel its smoothness and blandness. And now — as if it was a minor illness we were catching from one another — I realised that Edwin's face, too, had been swept clean of the emotions so inadvertently revealed.

"Yes, isn't it great," he found himself able to say in response to the words which by now *I* found myself able to say: "Isn't it marvellous?"; "What a relief," and so forth.

There followed an uneasy silence — or what would have been silence if any one of the three of us had had the hardihood to turn off the set when the news came to an end. As it was, our assorted and secret thoughts churned in our separate skulls against a background of penguins stamping their feet to dance music — an advertisement for some kind of bank loan, I suppose.

Jason was the first to move, rising rather abruptly from his chair and murmuring something about homework. His departure made things worse, made things better: better because whatever awful things Edwin and I might be going to say to each other would now be safely out of our son's hearing: worse because we would now be more likely to say them.

In the event, nothing much was said at all.

"I suppose I should ring the Barlows," I ventured uncertainly, after having summoned up the nerve to switch off the television, our only remaining bulwark against having to say something.

"They'll be thrilled, won't they? I — we — must congratulate them."

"That's right. Do that thing. Congratulate them."

The words, forced out from between his teeth, stayed my hand as I reached for the telephone. How could I ring Daphne and Sally with Edwin hovering like this, radiating darkness and dismay where all should have been joy and light?

"Well . . . that is . . . perhaps not just now. They'll be too . . . that is . . ."

"What's their address? Give me their address," Edwin interrupted urgently, and I complied without arguing. Well, surprise that he didn't *know* their address hardly seemed relevant any longer. I didn't feel capable of being surprised at anything any more.

Not many moments later I heard the car starting up, and I could imagine how the rain must be lashing against the windscreen, just as it was lashing against these windows. It was only now that I noticed the weather had broken, and all I thought was, "What a shame, all those flowers beaten down and sodden, just when Richard is coming home in triumph."

CHAPTER IX

His stunning good looks were what I noticed first on meeting Richard Barlow. Tall, dark and handsome as any hero of any romantic novel, hair greying at the temples in the approved manner, he greeted me with impeccable courtesy, ushering me into the library and seating me in the large armchair facing the window. The sun no longer streamed in as it had done during my last visit: the view outside was one of grey and windswept dissolution, wet leaves everywhere, wet plants flopping across the beds, and bare twigs tossing to and fro in rainy gusts of wind.

My host, still punctilious in his hospitality, and entirely self-possessed in spite of the hideous embarrassment that surely lay ahead, was offering me a cigarette, a drink. I noticed that he limped slightly as he moved from desk to cupboard and back, but only when he finally sat down facing me did I see how pale he looked, and how strained. As well he might, for not only had he just returned from his prolonged ordeal, physical and mental, but he was about to embark on what must be one of the most difficult interviews of his whole journalistic career: an interview, that is, with the wife of a man caught red-handed perpetrating the most monstrous fraud, stringing the world's media along with a cock-and-bull story of truly gargantuan proportions.

He had thought it was going to be a shock to me.

"I am much afraid, Mrs Wakefield," he began, "that what I am about to reveal to you is going to be very, very painful, but . . ."

Painful yes. He can say that again. But a shock, no. It was

difficult, now, to pin down the exact moment when I had realised that Edwin was lying, that his whole story of his adventures in the desert was being made up out of the top of his head. Perhaps there wasn't an exact moment? Rather an accumulation of clues . . . of gaps and discrepancies in the narrative itself, culminating in that display of naked horror yesterday evening when the news came through that his two alleged companions were not, after all, either dead or held captive. Against all the probabilities, they were at large again, all agog (as any journalist would be) to publish a full account of their adventures, in the process of which they would inevitably be showing up Edwin as the unscrupulous liar that he was; a disgrace to his profession.

I listened, face averted and making no comments, while Richard Barlow gave me his account of what had happened, and it left no doubt at all that Edwin's story was a total fabrication. He hadn't been captured: he hadn't been incarcerated in any terrorist hide-out. He hadn't even gone on the trip with the other two journalists at all. He had been invited to come . . . he had agreed to come, and then at the last moment had backed out.

"Cold feet, I have to conclude," Richard observed with a contemptuous curl of the lip. "Too dangerous — and of course it *was* a dangerous assignment, we knew that from the start. Though in the event we were set upon not by terrorists, but by a gang of hoodlums set on stealing our cameras and equipment. Which in the end — being half a dozen against two — they succeeded in doing: after cracking a few bones, I have to say, and bashing old Leo unconscious. That's what held us up afterwards. He was flat out; I couldn't carry him — I wouldn't have dared try, what with all his broken bits and pieces — not to mention mine.

"No one came by all that day, and when we were finally picked up, by a couple of villagers with an ox-cart, there was still no telephone . . . no transport. It was quite a party, I assure you, and your hero husband wasn't involved in any of it. I'm afraid, Mrs Wakefield, that he was sitting comfortably in some anonymous little hotel somewhere concocting his story for his poor benighted editor — *International Focus*, isn't it? — and relying (mistakenly as it happily turns out) on us being either dead or permanently incarcerated, and thus unable to give him the lie. We were the only two people in the world who could have shown him up, and with us out of the way it looked as if he would get away with it.

"I'm sorry, Mrs Wakefield, it gives me no pleasure to have to talk to you like this about a one-time colleague, but I think you have to know."

He was right. I did have to. I had to prepare myself for what was going to happen next. Edwin's brief hour of glory was over. All those contracts for books, articles, TV appearances, films; all those headlines — FROM HOSTAGE TO HERO — EDDIE IS SAFE — SURVIVOR IN THE SAND — all this was at an end. From now on he would be a laughing-stock; he would sink not merely into oblivion, but into worse than oblivion. No editor, anywhere, would ever employ him in any capacity again. Among our friends he would never be able to hold up his head again.

"So—so now . . .?" I began. I wasn't quite sure what question I was trying to ask. I could see clearly enough the disgrace that was coming to us, but I felt bemused about what to expect en route? What *does* happen to journalists who turn in phoney copy on this sort of scale? Immediate exposure? Public humiliation on the world's media? Or would it be some more private death-blow? A condemnation from the Press Council? Or what?

"Well, as to that," said Richard, fiddling now with a paper-knife which he had picked up from the desk, "it rests entirely with me — and with Leo, of course, when he gets back to this country, which I'm afraid won't be for some days yet as they don't think he's ready to be moved. By which time, of course, the whole story will be stone-dead anyway. If I choose to do nothing, to play-down my own story, leaving out such bits of it as glaringly contradict your husband's, then nothing will happen. I suppose that is what you would wish?"

Was it? What did I wish, other than to sink through the floor and never have to face anything or anybody ever again?

Richard was continuing:

"I take it you have had no chance as yet to talk this over with your husband? He asked me not to tell you — begged me, I may say (here once more the scornful curl of the lip) — but that of course is ridiculous. Obviously, you have to know. As a loyal wife you will, of course, take his side, you will back up any story he chooses to tell, so that even a coward like him will have nothing to fear from your knowing the truth. I pointed this out to him, but I'm sorry to . . ."

At this point, I seemed to recover my power of speech.

"Wait!" I cried, "when did all this . . .? I mean how is it that you've been talking to Edwin already? There's been no time — !"

"My dear Mrs Wakefield, your husband *made* time, as the saying goes. He was on my doorstep when I arrived home at midnight, after a long exhausting journey. My wife was with me and we had hoped — indeed had expected and assumed — that we would get a few hours of peace when we reached home, but it was not to be. This distraught and insistent person, who had already blocked my driveway with his vehicle, was demanding absolute priority on my attention. Neither greeting my mother nor looking through my mail was permitted to take precedence . . .

"Now, where was I? Ah yes: your husband's request (a trifle impertinent, I felt, in the circumstances) — his request that his midnight visit to me, and our ensuing discussion, should be kept secret from you. As I say, I could countenance no such plan. 'Your wife has a right to know the truth,' I told him, and I further warned him that if he persisted in keeping it from you, then I would tell you myself. And what do you think he said?"

What indeed? I pondered. No use just going into a sulk, as he would have done at home if he didn't get his own way.

"I don't know — what did he say?" I asked feebly; and

68

watched the firm, resolute face in front of me flicker into a scornful smile.

"He said, Mrs Wakefield, he said; 'If you tell her, I'll kill you!' — and really, I had to laugh! The idea that a little ra — I'm sorry, I mean a man like him — that a man like him, who chickens-out of assignments because he's scared, is going to have the nerve to commit murder — well, it's ludicrous, isn't it? So, 'Go ahead!' I told him, 'Go ahead and plan your murder — and see what happens! You'll get cold feet when it comes to the point, and you won't do a thing.' Isn't that right, Mrs Wakefield? From what you know of your husband?"

Out of the depths of my humiliation, I felt a flicker of rebellion. I wasn't going to be got at like this, justifiable though Richard's anger assuredly was.

"If you mean that my husband isn't a man who would commit murder, then you are quite right," I was beginning, with some asperity; and at once his manner recovered its former suavity: he was the perfect host once more, apologising, smoothing over the worst of the awkwardness, and even inviting me to stay to lunch.

"My mother and my wife are expecting you," he explained, "and I wouldn't like them to be disappointed. Perhaps I should tell you that I have decided to tell them nothing of this unfortunate affair between me and your husband. As a matter of fact I have so far told nothing to anyone. I refused to give interviews until after I got home. My chief concern right now is not to upset my family. And they *would* be upset. Very much so. They already feel that you yourself are now a close friend of the family, and they would be much distressed if anything were to come about to destroy that friendship. Particularly Sally" — and as he spoke the name, a softness and a brightness came over the rather severe features, and one knew that here was a man in love — "I would be very sad indeed if this day — this *very* happy day for her — were to be spoiled by so sordid an imbroglio. And so, Mrs Wakefield, if you could find it in your conscience to say nothing to them about our conversation, and to continue behaving to them just as you have done hitherto, I would be most grateful.

"By the way, to alleviate any embarrassment you may be feeling in my company, let me assure you that I won't be present at this little lunch party. I have an appointment at one-fifteen (glancing at his watch) and shall be fully occupied all the afternoon. There is a lot to see to — and none of it made easier by your husband's machinations, I'm sorry to say. Enough of that, though; I don't intend ever again to refer to . . . Ah, Mother! Hello! I hope I'm not holding things up by keeping our guest chatting for too long . . ." and a minute later I was walking in Daphne's wake across the polished floor towards the dining-room.

CHAPTER X

The readiness with which human beings expand to fill the roles allotted to them has always amazed me. The callow youth gets dressed in the morning, and becomes a policeman. The hen-pecked husband unlocks the gate and becomes the Headmaster. The flustered elderly woman muddling her change in the supermarket walks up the road and becomes Granny. It is this quality, I suppose, which has allowed human beings to evolve as a social species at all, and so I don't know why I should have been so surprised to find myself partaking of it in full measure during that lunch time. Once in the company of Daphne and Sally, exposed on every side to their uncomplicated relief and joy, I found it impossible not to share in this mood of rejoicing. It was my role: I had been invited here to share it, and so share it I did, my recent distress and humiliation not exactly forgotten, but hovering ghost-like on the edge of my consciousness, rather like a severe pain for which one has taken pain-killers.

"You see?" Sally was exclaiming, laughter and pure happiness blended in her voice, "You see, I *said* he was going to be all right, and he *is*, isn't he? I felt it in my bones, I told you! I *kept* saying it, and you wouldn't believe me!"

"No, dear. And you were quite right, weren't you? How lucky we are!"

Clearly, Daphne was feeling too relieved and happy to allow the thing to turn into an argument: she was allowing her daughter-in-law an easy win. Because, of course, Sally's bones

71

hadn't really constituted evidence, and a lucky guess doesn't really argue a superior assessment of the situation.

Sally had simply been lucky.

Lucky, lucky, lucky.

"And we had *another* bit of luck, too," Sally was babbling on, "I don't suppose Richard told you, did he, Clare; he always makes light of anything at all dangerous — that's one of the things that's so marvellous about him, isn't it, Mother-I-mean-Daphne?"

"Well — up to a point," Daphne agreed, smiling, "though I must say I'd worry about him less on these trips if he'd . . ."

"But like I'm saying, this *wasn't* the trip!" Sally broke in, "This was on the way back from the airport! Would you believe it, Clare, after all that wildly dangerous stuff out in God-knows-where . . . and then to be within an inch of death when we're just nearly home! It's lucky he was the one driving, I'm sure *I'd* never have managed to . . ."

"Sally! Sally, darling! Poor Clare doesn't know *what* you're talking about! Do tell the story properly . . . Start at the beginning."

"Well, all right, but there *wasn't* a beginning, not really, it was all absolutely sudden. You see, we were bowling home along the High Road, just before you get to the church, when suddenly this madman drove out of a side road slap in front of us! Richard had to do an instant U-bendy sort of loop, right on to the wrong side of the road — if anything had been coming, we'd have had it, but luckily it's pretty quiet at that time of night, and so there's no harm done . . ."

"Well, a broken rear light and a lot of scratches, I wouldn't call that *no* harm," interposed Daphne. "Not to mention this lunatic — a drunken driver, one presumes — getting away scot-free! I do think, Sally, if only you'd had the presence of mind to note the number . . ."

"Oh, but Mother-I-mean-Daphne, how *could* I? It was so sudden, you've no idea. I didn't even know if we'd been killed until I found that we hadn't, if you see what I mean, and by the time the other car was clean away . . ."

The mild bickering was just beginning to cloud the occasion, when a timely diversion introduced by Barnaby forced the discourse into new channels.

"S'a caterpillar in my salad," he announced, with evident satisfaction. "S'a green one, all wriggling! . . . Yuck!"

Instant concern. Chairs scraped back, adult faces loomed over the child, one on each side, peering anxiously at his plate.

"Where, Barnaby?" "Show me!" "Where is it . . . ?"

"*There!*" His fork traversed a vague parabola above the food, randomly pointing. "S'there! Yuck!"

Careful search ensued.

"Now, Barnaby, don't be silly, there's nothing there; just delicious lettuce . . ."

"Barnaby, dear, you're imagining it, look again, you'll see there just *isn't* a . . ."

"Oh, well, I must've eatened it, then," hazarded the star of the show: and then, pathetically: "have I got to eat the rest?"

An ingenious choice of words: 'The rest of the caterpillars' would seem to be implied, and what mother — or grandmother — would be so heartless as to insist on this?

"Well . . ."

"Now look, Barnaby dear . . ."

The concerned voices wove in and out above his head, locked in familiar argument: "Why give him salad, dear, if he isn't going to eat it?" "Oh, but Mother, it's *good* for him. They all say . . ." "Yes, I daresay, but it's only good for him if he *eats* it. If you aren't going to make him eat it, then what's the point of . . .?"

"Oh, *Mother*! You should never *make* a child eat anything! That's just the way to set up food-phobias . . ."

"Yuck!" contributed Barnaby, "Yucky caterpillar dinner!" and pushing the offending vegetation so far to the side of his plate that it toppled over the edge, he sat back contentedly to watch his minions clearing up the mess, continuing as they did so to

73

discuss, in eminently reasonable tones, the ethical, physiological and educational issues involved.

It reminded me of Edwin, I don't know why. Just when I least wanted to be reminded of him. All too soon, I was going to have to go home and face him; face the despair, the fear, the humiliation which Richard Barlow's unanswerable accusations must inevitably have caused. I must face, too, the implications of something I had noticed earlier without attaching any significance to it — I mean, the scratches and the slight dent in the bonnet of our car. The damage was very minor — I couldn't even be sure it was new — and all I thought at the time was, I must ask Edwin about it. Now, all I thought was, I must *not* ask Edwin about it. I must get it repaired as quickly as possible, and never think about it again.

By the time I left, the rain had ceased, the sky had cleared, and the low autumn sun was blazing with uncanny brilliance right into my eyes, making a small hazard of every roundabout or side-road. How convenient, I found myself thinking at one point, if I *did* have a small, a very small accident, creating a few fresh scrapes, one or two minor dents, among which the existing ones could merge without trace. Not that these reflections did anything at all to alleviate my natural motorist's alarm at each individual hazard as I encountered it. I have read that it is often like this for suicides, too: on their way to the high jump, they will still spring in terror from the path of an oncoming bus: on preparing to slit their wrists they will still concern themselves with whether or not the carving knife is clean.

With every stage of the journey, my reluctance to actually reach home mounted: soon, I was crawling along at a pace which won me hoots of annoyance and derision from every side, and I began to realise that I was faced with two options: either to arrive home, or to stop now.

Not far from where we live, there is a park abutting on a small stretch of woodland not yet demolished by the developers. Thither I made my way, and having parked the car by the main entrance I set off towards the trees with the vague feeling that among those silver-birch trunks gleaming wetly in the last of the sunshine, I would be able to set my thoughts in order, and know what was the right thing to do.

'As a loyal wife, you will of course take your husband's side,' Richard Barlow had said: and I envied him the rigid code from which this remark had sprung. If only I, too, had the guidance of some moral principle, no matter how blinkered, bigoted and prejudiced, from which it would be impossible for me to deviate. Other principles came into my mind, more ancient by far than Richard's: like that passage in the Jewish funeral service for a deceased wife, where the bereaved husband declares:

'She did me good and not evil all the days of her life.'

What *was* the good that at this juncture I could do to Edwin? And what the evil? Simply taking his side, encouraging him to stick to his false story, assuredly might not be doing him good: but on the other hand, refusing to take his side, insisting on showing him up as the liar that he was — would not this assuredly be doing him evil? It would look like it, certainly. And what *is* evil, anyway? At least half of it *consists* of what it looks like, and of what it feels like to the victim.

I was deep among the trees now, the gleams of sunlight on the wet trunks were gone, and I looked around, vaguely, for somewhere to sit. I could think better — or thought I could — if I was sitting down.

But everywhere was wet, so wet. Every tempting log was slushy with moss and lichen, the floor of the woodland was awash with sodden leaves. I must keep walking, then, but slowly . . . slower . . . and soon I was leaning up against the ancient drooping branch of an ancient dying oak, and staring into a quietness broken only by the faint drip-drip from some twig or dead leaf saturated beyond its power of absorption in the moist air. Large, luscious fungi, the most silent form of vegetation ever evolved, shared with me the great dying bough, sucking nutrients from the sodden bark.

Why, *why* had Edwin concocted this elaborate, this preposterous falsehood? What had he hoped to gain? Perhaps this was putting the question the wrong way round: it wasn't anything he had hoped to gain so much as something he was desperately seeking not to lose: namely, his self-respect as a professional journalist, as well as all the glory and glitter of his new-found fame.

Knowing him as I did, and over so many years, I could see exactly how it had come about. He had been thrilled — yes, he had been genuinely thrilled — at being assigned to this trip. He had seen real success — yes, and fame — within his grasp at last, and on making the final arrangements with his prospective colleagues he had, I am certain, intended to fulfil his part in the enterprise.

And then, as the time for setting off drew near, and as the dangers inherent in the undertaking bit deeper and deeper into his imagination — well, as Richard Barlow had put it, he got cold feet. He had panicked, and had done the unforgivable thing for an investigative journalist; he had lost his nerve and backed out, letting down his colleagues, his editor, and disgracing himself for ever in his profession.

Even so, how had he come to venture on this ludicrous farrago of lies, any or all of which his two putative colleagues could disprove in a moment?

Well, no, they couldn't, could they, as things seemed to be turning out? The rumours, followed by the apparently definitive news, that Richard and Leo had been captured and probably killed, must have seemed to let him off the hook entirely, and must have inspired him to invent his own face-saving story, which could now (in all probability) never be questioned, and on the crest of which he could now ride not merely to acceptance, but to all the dazzle of fame which had been his original motive for embarking on the whole enterprise.

Simple, I saw it all. And so this was the man I must go home to this evening. A coward, a liar, a betrayer of his colleagues. And, incidentally, a total and disgraceful failure in his chosen career.

Well, not incidentally. It's being a failure that turns a person into a liar and a coward, not the other way round. Looking back now, in the deepening twilight of the wood, I thought about what Edwin had done to himself over the years. He had seen himself all along as a man he simply wasn't — a man of courage, stamina and iron will-power — and had landed himself in a career which demanded these qualities to an extreme degree. When the crunch came, and these exalted qualities failed him, his only resource was lying and cheating.

And hadn't it been the same at home? He had embarked happily enough on fatherhood, possessing only the modest skills required for getting on with a toddler, or perhaps with a small, admiring five- or six-year old: and then, later, when confronted by a creature taller than himself, better at fixing the video, and with the whole world still ahead of him instead of half of it already behind — caught in such a predicament, what could a frightened man do other than try desperately to belittle the burgeoning creature, to rubbish its encroaching powers?

I thought about those marks, still visible on the kitchen door, with which we, proud parents, had once recorded the growth of our small son, giving no thought at all to the direction in which those marks were unstoppably leading.

The silence seemed to thicken in the damp, darkening air, and I felt inexpressibly alien in this secret world of vegetation moving harmoniously towards its long sleep. Me, I was irreversibly awake, a creature so constituted that it must constantly move about, must do things, must decide on a course of action or against a course of action: if not this, then that . . .

A sudden stirring of the undergrowth only a few feet away shot through my body like a flash of lightening: complex moral decisions vanished, the options reduced to the utter clarity of fight or flight.

But only for a second. Less than a second.

"Mum!" exclaimed Jason, pushing through the tangle of dripping foliage, shaking the loose wetness from his hair. "What on earth are you . . . ? The chap at the gate said he'd seen a lady on her own coming down this way, and so I . . . Look, Mum, for Pete's sake come home! Dad's doing his nut about the car . . . !"

My shoulders had grown so stiff from leaning so long against the wet branch, it was quite difficult to propel myself upright; but I made it.

"*What* about the car?" I asked, my mind a turmoil of evasion and anxiety. Something about those dents and scratches . . . ? Hell, I was becoming quite paranoic about them! Surely, if my suspicions were well-founded, this was the *last* subject Edwin would be likely to raise with his young son.

"Just that it's not there, and he doesn't know where it's gone. I started trying to tell him that I'd seen it on my way home from school, parked safe and sound, by the gate here, but . . . Oh, *you* know, Mum, what Dad's like when he gets things into his head! Worries them to pieces like a terrier, and then bites your head off if you try to help any . . . So anyway, I thought I'd retire temporarily from the line of fire, and come to suss it out for him.

"And so here I am. Behold, you're sussed. And so . . ." Suddenly his voice changed: "Mum! I say! D'you know what you've got there? Look — just by your right foot — don't move! It may be only a boletus, but it's a fantastic size. I wonder if . . . I must show it to Tim, he'll know . . . "

Taking a couple of steps forward, he bent down and very gently detached the yellowish, bloated thing from its moorings, and then stood, uncertainly, cupping it in both hands.

"I ought to have brought a tin, or something," he lamented, moving the thing cautiously from one palm to the other, "It'll be a tragedy if I let it get broken before Tim sees it."

Tim Fergusson, bespectacled, ginger-haired and very polite was one of the most assiduous visitors to our household after school, and I had lately become aware of the lad's craze for mycology, as a result of the hitherto unknown Mrs Fergusson's increasingly urgent telephone calls asking me to check whether our *Edible Fungi of the British Isles* saw eye to eye with her *Why Only Mushrooms?* in respect of the particular specimen that her son was on the point of frying in butter for the family's evening meal. So far, Jason's more theoretical interest in the subject hadn't extended to this sort of thing, and I could only hope that this remarkable specimen, plump as a doughnut and twice the size, wasn't going to prove an inspiration to culinary experiment. I knew very well what the *Edible Fungi* book would say — it would declare the ugly thing to be not only edible, but 'delicately flavoured' — all that sort of thing, for all the world like an advert for vintage wine.

I observed, uneasily, the loving way he cradled the specimen in both hands, walking gingerly among the slippery ruts of the woodland path so as not to jolt it.

That's all I needed for my encounter with Edwin tonight — a teenage son frying fungi for our supper. It crossed my mind to ring up Mrs Fergusson and beg her to ring back and say that *her* book said that the boletus was deadly poisonous: but something — a sort of moral weariness rather than a real moral scruple — restrained me. To get involved in *another* web of lying was too much; my whole soul shrank from it in exhaustion.

CHAPTER XI

"Where have you been? Why didn't you tell me?"

Because you were still asleep when I left. Because I knew it would make you furious, and I didn't see why we should have two rows where one would do: the one we'll be having now I'm back will be plenty.

And, above all, because I can't think what in the world to say to you now that I know for certain that you've been lying, that your whole story has been a fabrication from beginning to end. Well, I'd known it for quite a while, actually, but all the while no one else knew, it was a sort of ghost-knowledge; ordinary day-to-day life could just walk through it as if it wasn't there.

But not any longer. Now that Richard Barlow knew, and I knew that he knew, and Edwin knew that I knew that he knew, no further pretence was possible between us. And without pretence, what was there? For a couple like us, I mean?

I looked across at Edwin and my heart sank. Indeed, the whole setting within which we were confronting each other was conducive to foreboding. We were in Edwin's study, the untidiness of which was tonight dismally aggravated by the glare of the single unshaded bulb dangling from the ceiling. He hadn't even switched on the electric fire against the chill of the October evening — a sure sign, if one was needed, of trouble to come. When Edwin is in one of his bad moods, the first thing he does is to cocoon himself in as many minor discomforts as he can assemble at short notice; I suppose to attract pity, though in fact pity is the very thing that seems to infuriate him most on such occasions. No good, then, to fling my arms round his neck crying, "Oh, Edwin, darling, how perfectly awful for you, I'm terribly, terribly sorry, I can just imagine how you're feeling." Any such display would have been worse than useless.

Or would it? I've sometimes wondered, since: but anyway, I didn't do it, and so we'll never know. Instead, I simply answered his questions, as coolly as I could.

"I think you know where I've been, Edwin. I've been to see Richard Barlow. He's told me everything, including the details of your visit to him last night. So now we know. You've been rumbled. The balloon's gone up; the cat's out of the bag. We have to think how to face it."

I paused. In a way, the worst was already over: I had broached the subject.

Edwin made no response. His face, lined and almost old in the harsh light was quite blank of expression, and I went on talking. A weird rush of exhilaration was making my words flow freely, and I found myself launched on a torrent of off-the-cuff condolences.

"But you know, Edwin, it's not the end of the world—that is, it needn't be. People have come home with tall stories, travellers' tales, before now; since the beginning of time, actually, and right up to the present day. Why, it's almost common! Look at that chap who pretended to have sailed round the world single-handed when actually he'd been coasting up and down off the Isle of Wight, or somewhere. Or that chap in the earthquake disaster, who claimed to have been buried under rubble for twenty-six days, when in fact nothing had happened to him at all and his home was quite undamaged, but he felt he'd missed out on the publicity. And then the Piltdown Skull, of course."

"What the hell is all this in aid of?" Edwin shouted, whirling round in his swivel chair and confronting me face-to-face for the first time. "Why are you wittering on like this about cheats and liars? Of course there have been cheats and liars, all through history. So what?"

81

So, you're in good company, is what I'd intended to convey; but clearly I'd put a foot wrong. Which foot? What *should* I have said? I started again:

"Look," I said, "let's get it straight. I've just had this long talk with Richard Barlow, and he's told me everything. Now, we have to decide what to do about it. Obviously he's angry, you can't wonder at that, but he did imply that he had no intention of giving you away, and so — "

"*Him* giving *me* away! I like that! That's rich, that's really rich! First he tells the most outrageous and implausible lies, accusing me to my face of having chickened-out on the trip; and then out of the kindness of his heart he offers not to tell on me! Come off it, Clare, don't tell me that *you* were taken in by his libellous nonsense! *You*, of all people . . ."

My head was spinning. Everything had gone into reverse. I felt as Newton would have felt if the apple had started lifting itself off the ground and settling itself back on the twig. What would have happened then to gravitation, to the Inverse Square Law . . . ?

I must hang on to my common sense. Above all, I must hang on to the facts. One of the facts was that well before my fatal interview with Richard Barlow, I had already realised that there was something badly wrong with Edwin's story. Both his behaviour and the discrepancies in his account of his adventures had forced me to the conclusion that he must be lying. Richard Barlow's revelations merely corroborated what I knew in my heart already.

"The two-faced double-crossing swine!" Edwin was blustering. "He's counting on getting his version into the heavies in preference to mine, because that's where he's got the pull — he's older than I am, better-known than I am . . . He's going to pull rank to get my story rubbished! Just because he's at the top of this racket, and I'm a mere beginner . . ."

A beginner? After twenty years or so? "Because he's a success and you're a failure," would be nearer to the harsh truth, but of course I said no such thing; and anyway, Edwin was still talking, warming to an indignation which was fast ceasing to be phoney. Was I witnessing the very early stages of that well-known phenomenon, the liar slowly, bit by bit, coming to believe his own lies?

"He thinks he can make a monkey of me, but mark my words, he's got another think coming! He thinks he's got me over a barrel because of the lack of independent evidence; he's banking on it being just my word against his . . ."

"But, Edwin," I could not help interrupting, "it's *not* just your word against his. Leonard Coburn was there too, remember. I know the doctors aren't allowing him to be questioned at the moment, but as soon as he's well enough . . ."

"That won't prove a thing!" His head jerked up, and I could hear in his voice the familiar gleeful lift-off as he soared towards what seemed to him a clinching argument: "you forget, Clare, that Leo is supposed to have had concussion. In a coma, one of the reports said. Who's going to trust the memory of a man just out of a coma? Everyone knows that concussion affects the memory — it blots out everything that happened before the accident, sometimes there's a blank of hours and hours. So if he starts saying I wasn't with them on the trip — well, it'll just be that he's forgotten! Post-traumatic amnesia. Anyone with any medical knowledge at all knows about *that*."

He'd just looked it up in the *Medical Dictionary*, anyone could tell. Certainly Richard Barlow would have been able to tell if Edwin had in fact brought up this same argument during their colloquy last night.

Had he? I hoped, for his sake, that he had *not*, because if ever a man had condemned himself out of his own mouth, this was what Edwin had done in leaping so prematurely on to Leonard Coburn's putative amnesia as a weapon on his, Edwin's, side. For it implied, did it not, that Edwin was already assuming that Leonard's story when he came out of his coma was going to tally with Richard's; had there been any likelihood that it would tally with Edwin's, then the amnesia argument would never have come up at all.

I felt a great sadness. Edwin wasn't even any good at this sort of thing. And the sadness went deeper than that, much deeper. I realised now for the first time how very much during these last hours I had been looking forward to sharing Edwin's secret, terrible though it was. It was years since we had shared anything: our many and various troubles had invariably divided us; had found expression in bad temper, evasion, and bickering. Not once, in the last decade or so, had we sat down to face something together, talked it over fully and freely, and decided, jointly, what to do about it. Not once: and during the last few hours I realised I had been indulging a fantasy that just this was going to happen at last. Edwin was going to confide in me about everything; about his lies, about the fear that had led up to them. How he had started off by longing for the fame and professional advancement that this hazardous venture was likely to have brought him; and how, when it came to the crunch, sheer terror had overcome him, and he had 'chickened-out'. Which, of course, brought with it the almost greater terror of irreversible disgrace and humiliation. At which desperate moment, the news of the capture of his two colleagues had seemed to provide a heaven-sent opportunity, a more or less foolproof way out of his predicament. Provided that they were either dead or subjected to prolonged incarceration (and experience with former hostages suggested that one of these two would prove to be the case), then all he had to do was to make up his own story and stick to it. A simple exercise in lying; one lie leading to another, of course, and then another, as is the way of lies.

But in the event, it wasn't working out like that; the whole thing had been blown sky-high by the wholly unexpected return of Richard Barlow, safe and sound.

All this, Edwin was going to confide in me, and together we were going to decide what to do.

This, anyway, was my fantasy, and it included myself in the star part of the fantasy wife: sympathetic, non-judgmental, infinitely wise; a wife who understood all, forgave all, and proved

84

herself a tower of strength to support him through the inevitable showdown when it came. I had even decided what I was going to say, what advice I was going to give. I would point out that it would be, at worst, a nine-days' wonder in the Press; everyone would soon lose interest, and he would then be able to live down the disgrace; even, perhaps, to salvage some paradoxical advantages from it. The headlines, for instance:

THE GREAT KIDNAP HOAX
EDDIE AND THE PINCH OF SALT!
PULL THE OTHER ONE, EDDIE!

These were the kind of headlines I was going to predict for him, facetious to the point of good-humour. And I truly think that this is how they would have been, in the tabloids, anyway; because, after all, deep in its black heart, the world loves a failure. Through all the shock-horror condemnations, the love shows. All this I was going to point out to him, and as, under my ministrations, he began to feel a bit better, I was going to tease him about the cartoons we were going to see: The notorious Eddie crouched over his typewriter knocking out a piece for the Editor of *THE WHOPPING LIAR* — that sort of thing. In the end, he would have to laugh a little, just as the world would be laughing . . . Bit by bit, he might end up as a folk hero, patron saint of the tall story, and a new verb 'to Eddiefy' could come into the language, not, of course, to be confused with 'edify'.

All this, and more, I was preparing myself to expound when the whole thing was flung back in my face by Edwin's startling insistence on sticking to his implausible lies, even with me. Instead of a shared problem, us against the world, there gaped between us now an abyss of pretence and counter-pretence. I must pretend to believe in him: he must pretend to believe that I believed in him . . . Where did he think this would get us? What did he expect me to say? More important, what did I expect *myself* to say?

A great weariness came over me, and I think over Edwin too. We both fell silent. He moved restlessly in his chair, put his hands over his eyes as if the light was hurting them.

Lies are tiring, no doubt about it. They require a life-support system which must never be switched off. They must be monitored constantly, you are never off duty: no wonder Edwin looked so lined and tired.

"I'll make some tea," I suggested — this being the most non-committal proposal I could think of at short notice — and hurried off to the kitchen before Edwin could think up a way of making the issue a controversial one. And as it turned out, this was a lucky move on my part, as it meant that it was I, not Edwin, who was confronted by that wretched toadstool thing — I'd already forgotten its name — lying in a pie-dish in the very centre of the kitchen table, as if on display. Hastily, I shoved it out of sight behind the breadbin. Why the sight of it would so certainly have upset Edwin I couldn't for the moment work out: I just knew that it would. In the same way, I suppose, as our primitive ancestors knew for certain that the sun would rise tomorrow without knowing anything at all of the forces which make the earth spin on its axis; without, indeed, knowing that the earth is spinning at all. So easy is it to come to an entirely correct conclusion from an entirely fallacious line of reasoning: but this, of course, only becomes clear with hindsight.

CHAPTER XII

I am lying alongside a murderer who has not yet committed a murder.

The thought came to me out of the darkness, utterly unannounced. Indeed, I might even have been dreaming, though I felt as if I hadn't been asleep at all throughout the long-drawn-out reaches of the night.

You know how it is with insomnia. Right there in the centre of your brain is a scrunched-up ball of barbed wire, about the size of a clenched fist, and on this your thoughts impale and entangle themselves, and cannot escape. They are not amenable to reason, nor to relaxation techniques. They didn't ask to be there in your head, any more than you asked to have them; but there they are, and you have to make the best of each other.

Murderers who have not yet committed a murder. All murderers are like that to start with, of course, even Jack the Ripper, and so what is the change that comes over them, between one moment and the next, which turns them from commonplace citizens into murderers?

"He always seemed such a nice, ordinary fellow, just like anybody else," the neighbours say afterwards. And of course that's what he was, because he wasn't a murderer before it happened, he *was* an ordinary fellow. So what was it that happened to change him, so quickly and so completely, in a minute or less? No other change in Nature is as quick as that . . .

87

The caterpillar into the chrysallis . . . The tadpole into the frog . . . it always takes quite a while — days, usually, or at least hours . . .

Tadpoles . . . Caterpillars . . . Coiled green things, black wriggling things, squirming and writhing behind my closed lids, interweaving, separating, winding in and out of one another in a slow, curving rhythm . . .

I thought I was falling asleep, but no such luck. My eyes had snapped open again, and there once more was the dim outline of the window behind the thin curtains, squared-off against the darkness of the room, and perceptibly brighter than it had been when I last looked. It couldn't be morning yet; it must be the moon, gibbous in the eastern sky, with its back tilted towards the coming dawn. A thin, a wafer-thin slice of silvery light fell across Edwin's bed from the crack between the curtains; and, propping myself on one elbow, I watched it moving, millimetre by millimetre, towards his face.

I hoped it wouldn't wake him; indeed, I was almost sure it wouldn't. After all the turmoil of the day, not to mention the harrowing conversation we had engaged in last night, he was sleeping as peacefully as a baby.

Is this how murderers normally sleep, the night before the deed? Or was Richard Barlow right? I recalled the scornful twist of the lip with which he had affirmed that my husband would never dare to commit a murder. 'He'd get cold feet. He'd chicken-out!'

Would he? I recalled the definition of a neurotic which I had read somewhere: 'A neurotic is a criminal without the courage to commit a crime.'

Was Edwin a neurotic? His bad moods . . . his anxieties . . . his endless fusses about everything . . . did it add up to neurosis? And anyway, was there any truth in the definition? How would you set about testing it?

I wondered, vaguely, why that streak of moonlight was taking so long to reach Edwin's face: then realised I'd had my eyes shut for some time now, and so that must be why I hadn't seen it happen.

Never mind. Soon it would be morning. Maybe everything would seem different in the morning?

CHAPTER XIII

The first thing that was different was that I overslept. It was past nine when I opened my eyes on the busy little alarm clock which had failed to wake me at a quarter-past seven, and when I got downstairs I found that Jason had done his own breakfast — some kind of a fry-up, from the look of it — and had got off to school. Edwin — wearing clean shirt, tie, and his most important-looking suit — was slumped over the breakfast table, surrounded by crumbs and marmalade, and scowling over a dauntingly bulky array of morning papers, both quality and tabloid.

He did not look up when I came in, and I stood for a moment assessing the clues before I risked upsetting him by saying 'Hullo', or 'Good Morning', or something similarly controversial.

The suit and the tie were the most unnerving of the clues. Normally, Edwin eats his breakfast in his tattered dressing gown and down-at-heel slippers. On the other hand, the crumbs and marmalade were a *good* sign: when he is in a *really* bad mood he has only a mug of black coffee, which he leaves untouched for long enough to be able to complain of it being cold. The significance of all those papers, though — that was more difficult: except for the fact that he must have gone out and bought them before breakfast, on his own two feet . . .

"The cunning swine!" he burst out, still without raising his head to look at me. "Hardly more than a couple of column inches

90

anywhere! What the devil's he up to? If he's trying to show me up, then all he had to do was to get *his* story splashed across the front pages! What's he holding back for? Here — look!" He pushed across the table towards me one of the more responsible dailies, jabbing with his thumb at a smallish item on one of the inner pages. *Second Journalist Safe Home*, was the non-sensational heading, in small bold, followed by a low-key and very short summary of the bare facts of Richard's experiences, carefully making no reference to the presence or absence of Edwin at any stage of the expedition. I read it twice, and it was clear to me that so cleverly were the discrepancies played down that no ordinary reader would be likely to deduce from it that Edwin's earlier and highly-publicised account was in direct conflict with this one. Richard must have deliberately foregone a lot of publicity due to himself in order to achieve this effect. A decent man, I surmised, behaving decently towards a colleague in the profession, and abiding punctiliously by the 'don't tell tales' ethos of the public school education to which he had assuredly been subjected.

"Well," I said warily, handing the piece back, "at least he's kept his word. He told me he had no intention of showing you up, and you must admit he's stuck to his promise so far. And at some cost to himself. I mean, he had a scoop on his hands if he'd have liked to use it . . ."

This whole speech was a mistake, especially the last bit. Never, ever, should you let yourself be trapped into enumerating the virtues of your husband's rival; each one is a red rag to a bull.

I had been about to seat myself at the marmaladey table to help myself to a slice of something, but now I decided to remain on my feet, the better to withstand the storm.

"'At some cost to himself'! 'A scoop on his hands!' Really, Clare, I don't know how you can be so naïve! Can't you see what he's up to? He's biding his time, he's getting his act together to smash me! Tomorrow — the next day — next week, you'll see the banner headlines in every paper accusing me of being a liar and a fraud! He'll get his scoop all right, don't you worry, and after all the publicity I've had, it'll be a big one!

"He's busy setting it up right now — can't you tell? He's up to something, I know he is! Haven't you noticed, Clare, that the media are beginning to drop me? That's *his* doing, it's obvious. Do you realise there wasn't a single call from the TV people all yesterday? Not even from radio. I don't know what strings he's been pulling to get me dropped — the Old Boy Network I suppose — but the fact remains that from the moment he set foot in this country, everything has stopped for me. Do you know, they didn't mention me on the News *at all* this morning? I listened at seven, and again at eight. Not a dickey-bird! They've *dropped* me, Clare. He's been getting at them, and they've dropped me like a hot brick! But, my God, he's not getting away with it! He'll find a hotter brick than he's ever bargained for dropping in *his* direction before he's much older!"

The pain, the outrage in Edwin's voice were almost laughable. Did he really imagine that Richard was responsible for the fading of his, Edwin's, newsworthiness? How long had he *thought* it was going to last, all this lionising and razzmatazz? He, of all people, should be aware of how swiftly even major world events drop out of the headlines and are seen on the news stands no more. The experience of Fame is almost a religious one, straight out of the Bible: 'He cometh up like the grass and is cut down.'

But this was hardly the moment to point this out. I could feel my mind filling up, like a cistern, drip, drip, drip, with less than tactful remarks. Sooner or later, one of them was going to overflow; and sooner (not later) one of them did.

"Well, but remember, Edwin, we were both out for a lot of yesterday, there could easily have been the odd call . . ."

Here I stopped, for two reasons. First, that 'the odd call' might sound a disrespectful sort of phrase by which to refer to so momentous an occurrence as a request for Edwin's participation in the *Bright and Early Chat Show*, or some such: second, I didn't want to reactivate our long-standing dispute over the installing, or not installing, of an answerphone. Pro (Edwin's argument): the possibility that important work opportunities for him might be lost if not responded to promptly: Con (mine): the fact that Edwin never responded promptly to work opportunities anyway, even when he *was* in to take the call.

Not that this last consideration applied at the moment. Since his sudden elevation to world stardom, he had been hanging over the phone like a love-sick teenager; but this wouldn't go on for ever; certainly not long enough to cover the time-span between the initial request for the instrument and the date when the final batch of technicians had tramped through our house for the last time, and the thing was actually installed.

And then, after all that, the part I dreaded most would begin: the duty (and assuredly it would fall on me) of apologising to all these callers for Edwin not having done a thing about them. If we *did* have an answerphone, I found myself thinking, then the recorded message should go something like this:

"If I don't take any notice of your call it'll be because I'm bored to death with you and can't be bothered to answer. So please don't waste your time ringing again."

Strange how swiftly such a series of desultory thoughts can flash through one's mind. I'll swear that there was no perceptible break in the sentence ending with "the odd call" before I was headlong into making amends, "A call from the TV people, I mean — something like that. Or maybe from *International Focus*? Which reminds me, Edwin, there's been another message for you from the editor. He's been trying to get hold of you ever since you got back . . ."

"The hell he has! Tell him to stuff himself, Clare! I've got bigger fish than *him* to fry, as he should realise by now. When he saw that screed in the *Daily Recorder*, he must have known that I . . ."

For a moment his face had lit up with the contemplation of past — well, two-day-old — glories; then it darkened.

"That's another thing, Clare! I don't like his tone! I couldn't understand it at first, but now I can see what's happened. This precious Richard of yours has been getting at him. He's gone behind my back to make trouble between me and my editor — don't you think that's a pretty rotten way for a fellow-journalist to behave? Don't you think so, Clare? You talk about his public school ethos — and perhaps that *is* the public school ethos? To betray your colleagues? To make trouble for them behind their backs? — If so, give me the secondary moderns any day . . ."

"They don't have secondary moderns any more," I pointed out, abandoning all attempts to placate. "And what's more, you're being very unfair, Edwin. There's absolutely no evidence that Richard has even heard of your editor, let alone telling tales to him about you. Why on earth should he? Why should he be doing *any* of these things? You seem to think he's trying to rubbish you — but *why*? What for? What does he stand to gain?"

"Listen, Clare, you're so innocent it's not true! I suppose it's the sheltered life I make it possible for you to lead; you have no conception of the jungle of treachery and back-biting and stabs-in-the-back within which *I* have to make my way. What does he stand to gain, you ask me? I'll tell you what he stands to gain. I'll tell you exactly what his long-term plan is. He plans to blackmail me. This killing of my story is only a start; the threats are going to follow. He'll threaten to show me up as a liar, and there'll be nothing I can do about it because he's at the top of this racket and holds all the strings. I'll be in his pocket, he thinks, and he'll be able to use me for any dirty business he likes, under threat of 'telling on me' if I refuse . . ."

Here he sprang to his feet, pushing back his chair with a loud crunching sound, pulverising toast crumbs and gouging yet further dents and scratches into the kitchen lino.

"What sort of a man do you think I am, Clare, to give in to that kind of a filthy threat? Knowing that it's all lies? And it *is* all lies, this preposterous story of my not having been there . . . surely you realise that? I did think, Clare, that you at least would have faith in me . . ."

Faith. A slippery concept. Somewhere, I once read of a schoolboy's definition of the word:

'Faith is believing in something that you know isn't true.'

I paused for just a second before answering. Then:

"Of course I do," I said.

CHAPTER XIV

It was only after he had left the house, with the familiar flurry of lateness, mislaid briefcase and complaints of never having time for a proper breakfast, that I found myself wondering what, exactly, he was late for? Our breakfast time quarrel — disputation — whatever you like to call it — hadn't been conducive to chatting about the day's programme.

He was going somewhere of significance, that was for sure; not lightly did Edwin get properly dressed before breakfast. Though of course during the last few days all his lifetime habits had been turned upside down, and at the beckoning of the media he would have rushed anywhere, at any hour, and wearing anything, even a suit.

But his brief hour of glory was at an end. On his own admission, no one in the publicity world had asked him to do anything, or be anywhere, since the night before last. He was yesterday's hero; today's dead duck, buried deep under a mountain of fresh happenings. The world had moved on without him, and this morning he was of less importance than even the tiniest happening in even the remotest corner of the world, so long as it was happening *now*.

So, it wasn't renewed media attention which had got him up so early. Nor was it a new offer from any of the publishers and editors who had made vaguely encouraging noises to him during the last few days. If it had been something like that, he would certainly have told me. Because, despite our damaging differences, and the gulfs of misunderstanding that lay between us, there was one area in which Edwin always kept touchingly close; and this was the area of his successes, insofar as there were any. A fan letter from a reader; a kind word from one of his editors; an appreciative mention of one of his articles, and he would be rushing to me like a child out of school with a good report. The kind words would be read out to me not once but half a dozen times; the appreciative mention would be xeroxed so that I might have a copy of my very own, to keep. And keep them I did, though *where* to keep them was a continuing problem. Some of them were currently in the dresser drawer among the tea towels; the one from Japan, as yet untranslated, still languished behind the tea-caddy, awaiting categorisation.

"A place for everything, and everything in its place," my grandmother used to say; but then she was married to my grandfather, not to Edwin.

It was disarming, in a way, this habit of his; it showed that he at least valued my admiration and approval. And the fact that he also valued absolutely *anybody's* admiration and approval didn't entirely devalue this little link between us. I don't know why, but it didn't.

So, it wasn't a lucrative offer of work from any source. What else might it be? What other errand might get a man out of the house at an unaccustomed time, dressed up to the nines, and carefully refraining from telling his wife where he was going?

An hour or so later, while I was still turning over the possibilities in my mind, the phone went: it was Sally.

"Oh, Clare!" she breathed excitedly, "your adorable husband is here — did you know he was coming? *We* didn't, it was just a lovely surprise. He's just popped in, he says, to see how we're getting on, isn't that darling of him? Mostly, I suppose, he wants to see Richard; they must have *such* a lot to talk about after all they've been through together, but unluckily Richard isn't here just at the moment. It's funny, he doesn't seem to be at the office either. I rang them, and apparently he hasn't been in at all this morning . . . something must have cropped up, I suppose . . ."

She paused; but before I had a chance to frame any of the questions that were taking shape in my mind, she was continuing:

"Anyway, I'm sure he'll be in to lunch . . . that's what I'm ringing about really, Clare. You see, it seems a shame that Edwin should miss seeing Richard altogether, after coming all this way, so I've asked him to stay to lunch; and then it occurred to me how nice it would be if you came too. I mean, since he's here anyway. And you could bring your car, Clare, couldn't you, so he wouldn't have that awful journey back on buses and things. It's ghastly crossing London by public transport, isn't it? Whenever I take Barnaby to the dentist I have to — our dentist's in Harley Street, you see; absolutely *nowhere* to park . . ."

It's always hard to break into Sally's telephone monologues, but I managed it this time. Sheer surprise made it easy:

"You mean Edwin hasn't come in the car? He's come all that way without it — in the rush-hour?"

Most un-Edwin-like behaviour, this. On top of the suit, and the briefcase, and the whole carry-on at breakfast.

"Wait a moment," I said, and going to the window I looked out. She was quite right: he hadn't taken the car.

Mystery after mystery. Perhaps I *had* better accept this invitation, if only to see what on earth was going on?

First, though, I was going to finish tidying the kitchen, having once started it; and so, telling Sally I'd be there soon after twelve, I returned to my task.

It wasn't as bad as it sometimes is. The biggest problem always is the assortment of unsolicited paper that litters every surface: free newspapers, free-gift advertisements and brochures, and all those miscellaneous brown envelopes which one can tell at a glance are not worth opening, and yet which make one feel uneasy at the thought of throwing them away.

Thank goodness the giant toadstool thing was gone, anyway. Jason must have remembered to take it to school with him to show to the knowledgeable Tim. With any half-way luck, the said Tim would take it to *his* home and keep it there, and then I wouldn't need to keep protecting Edwin from being upset by it. Maybe Tim's mother didn't have anyone who had to be protected from this sort of thing?

Lucky lady!

CHAPTER XV

The Indian summer had returned. Barnaby, who had hurried out of the front door at the sound of my car drawing up, now escorted me through a gate at the side of the house into a sunlit glory of green and gold and bronze. A wide lawn stretched before us, flanked by shrubs and tall trees ablaze with autumn colours, and in the centre of this glowing space Edwin reclined at ease in a red-and-white canvas deckchair. A tall glass of some sparkling drink stood on a wrought-iron table to his right, while on his left Sally was curled companionably on a rug, her laughing face tilted up towards him as if he had just made some exquisitely amusing joke. Edwin loves to feel that his jokes have been exquisitely amusing — well, I suppose we all do — and it was obvious to me that he was having the time of his life: though just how he had come by it was still obscure. Had he simply gate-crashed the little family? Or had one of them phoned him? Or what?

"S'not Daddy," Barnaby announced, marching purposefully up to the tranquil pair, "s'only Clare. So we can play 'Plink' some more, can't we Edwin? *'Plink'*" he repeated, with further emphasis, fixing an imperious gaze on Edwin. "*'PLINK'*". And then, prompting his laggard playmate: "You have to ask me, what does 'Plink' mean?"

"All right. What does 'Plink' mean?" Edwin asked obligingly without bothering to open his eyes — the sun was blazing full into his face, so one couldn't blame him — "Go on — what does 'Plink' mean?"

"It means I've got to run to the end of the garden and swing six swings in the swing and then run back," shrilled Barnaby, suiting the action to the word: but all too soon, and long before any adult conversation could be properly resumed, he was back again.

"'Grum'!" he squealed, "Edwin, Edwin, you have to ask me, What does 'Grum' mean?"

Apparently 'Grum' meant that Barnaby had to run to the shrubbery, fetch a red thing, a blue thing and a brown thing, and bring them back to us: which assignment being completed in about twelve seconds flat, I could see Edwin's patience coming swiftly to an end.

"What does 'Crig' mean? Why, it means you've got to run round and round the lawn four hundred times, and then sit still for an hour without speaking," Edwin pronounced sternly; and when, after a moment's bemused calculation, both Barnaby and his mother fell about laughing, he looked both startled and gratified. He had not anticipated so flattering a response to his intended *coup de grâce*.

"Oh, well, all right: *you* tell me what 'Crig' means," he conceded; and so the game went on, greatly to Barnaby's satisfaction, and to Edwin's too, I fancied, basking as he was in the glow of Sally's maternal approval.

"He's marvellous with children, your husband, isn't he?" she enthused during one of Barnaby's self-imposed sorties out of hearing. "It must have been wonderful for you when *your* son was small."

My heart twisted with nostalgic pain and with the pure unsullied envy I had felt more than once in Sally's presence. Because Edwin *had* been marvellous with Jason when he'd been this sort of age. The contrast between the father-son relationship of those days and the way it was now between the two of them was almost too much to be borne. I was jealous, jealous, jealous. Not (as some wives might have been) of my husband's chatting-up a lovely young woman in the sunshine, but of his effortless success with this child who was not ours, in contrast to his dark and damaging failure with the child who was.

Lunch time came, and still no Richard.

"It's really very odd," observed Daphne, ladling out some very good tomato soup flavoured with fennel, "He was so definite about being back in time for lunch. He has the last instalment of that *Changes in the Eastern Bloc* series to finish. I suppose . . ." she turned to Edwin — "he didn't say anything to *you*, did he, about his plans for today? I imagine that when you arranged to come here . . ."

"Oh, but Mother-I-mean-Daphne, Edwin came on impulse." Here she turned to me: "It was so funny, Clare, you know that path which runs along the bottom of all these gardens? Well, I was looking out of our bedroom window, watching Barnaby twirling himself around on the swing — he can't swing himself properly yet, you know; Richard's been trying to teach him, but . . ."

"I *can* swing myself properly!" interrupted Barnaby darkly, clashing his spoon ferociously against the rim of his plate. "That *was* properly, how I was swinging myself!"

"Yes, sweetie, yes, of course it was," Sally assured him hastily. "Yes, well, there he was, swinging himself properly, and suddenly I noticed a man watching him from over the hedge. Well, for a minute I was quite scared — you know — a strange man — one hears such awful things nowadays, I thought it might be a murderer or something, so I rushed downstairs . . . but it was all right, it wasn't a murderer at all, it was *Edwin!*"

She looked round the table, beaming. "He'd got lost, poor sweet, hadn't you, Edwin? He thought it was a short cut, a lot of people do, but actually you can't get into the gardens from that path at all, it only leads to the golf course, and to the Botanical Centre . . ."

"So Sally kindly directed me back on my tracks, and I was able to make a thoroughly respectable entry by the front gate — " Edwin took up the tale; and then, turning to Daphne: "No, I'm

102

afraid I *don't* know anything about Richard's movements. As Sally says, nothing was planned, I just came on spec. And how glad I am that I did . . . Such a delightful morning, in such delightful company . . ."

His spirits, I could see, were quite recovered from the breakfast-time gloom, and throughout the meal he and Sally kept up an increasingly flirtatious exchange of banter, highly entertaining to both, though less so, I could see, to Daphne, whose look of quiet disapproval deepened. Apart from a few polite remarks necessitated by her role as hostess, she spoke scarcely at all.

Only when we were alone together in the drawing-room after lunch — Sally and Edwin having undertaken jointly the apparently onerous task of settling Barnaby for his afternoon rest — did she put her unease into words.

"I do hope, Clare," she said, "that Sally's behaviour hasn't upset you? Do let me assure you, it doesn't mean a thing. She has this flirtatious way with her, but it's just high spirits really, and she does it with anyone when she's in the mood; it's part of her nature. She's like a child, you know, in many ways, and she doesn't always quite realise the impression she's making. I've tried to have a word with her now and again, but of course, as mother-in-law, I have to be so *very* careful. One must never, ever, seem to criticise. And of course, I do know that she's absolutely devoted to my son really. There's nothing actually to worry about . . ."

Here she glanced down, restlessly turning her wedding-ring round and round on her white, shapely finger.

"But all the same, I don't like outsiders getting a wrong impression. As mother-in-law you can't win. If you intervene . . . or if you don't intervene . . . it's difficult . . . One's solitary, well-meaning self pitted against the whole, vast Mother-in-Law as Interfering Monster image. And in my case it's further complicated by the fact that my son has chosen this rather hazardous profession and devotes himself to it heart and

103

soul. There are many occasions when I can't help worrying about him, but I mustn't show it, or talk about it, because Sally herself doesn't worry at all. She seems immune to anxiety in any shape or form, and so *my* worry comes across as a sort of mother-hen fussing. Right now, for instance, Richard not being back yet. Sally's not bothered in the least. 'Something's cropped up,' she says, and no doubt it has; but what? Apart from anything else, he's expecting several important phone calls today — there was one from Tokyo just before lunch, and they seemed very put out, in a Japanese kind of way, when I had to say he wasn't here . . .

"*I* don't know; perhaps I *do* worry too much. Perhaps, given the nature of Richard's job, it really is better to be like Sally. Actually, I think he loves her to be like that . . . I'm sure he does. A worrying kind of wife wouldn't suit him at all. Tell me, Clare, do *you* worry about your husband when . . . ?"

But our discussion of the pros and cons of worrying over our loved ones was abruptly halted by the crashing open of the drawing-room door by an outraged Barnaby, shoeless, and with flaxen curls tumbled all over his scarlet tear-stained face.

"'S'not fair!" he raged. "Granny, tell Mummy it's not fair! She says it's not three o'clock yet, and it *is* three o'clock . . . !"

By this time Sally too had appeared in the doorway, likewise somewhat dishevelled.

"Barnaby, you shouldn't come asking Granny the time when I've already *told* you the time. It's . . ."

"'Tisn't!"

For a moment, deadlock supervened. Neither of the adults seemed to know what to do next, though the ball was clearly in their court. By now, I had divined the nature of the dispute: Barnaby's afternoon rest was scheduled to last until three o'clock, and here he was, at barely half-past two, throwing down the gauntlet.

"Now, look, Barnaby . . ."

"Barnaby dear, don't you think you'd better . . ."

104

"Listen, Barnaby, if you'll come and finish your rest like a good boy, then when you get up you can have a . . ."

"Sally, dear, are you sure it's a good idea, bribing him with . . ."

The controversy being thus raised to the more lofty heights of the moral and ethical issues involved in child-rearing, Barnaby's tears dried on the instant. His eyes darted with professional aplomb from one to the other of the disputants, like a spectator at a tennis match. He didn't mind who won, the game was the thing, every second taking them nearer and nearer to the witching hour when afternoon rests come to an end.

Game, set and match to Barnaby. By ten to three, it was obviously not worth while to force, lure or bribe him back to his bed; and so here we all were, out in the sunshine again, Sally sprawled on a rug and Edwin, sitting cross-legged at her side being, at Barnaby's insistence, the Prince to her Sleeping Beauty. An easy role while it lasted, for whenever the small producer tried to introduce some action into the scene, he was sharply reminded by the leading man that the princess had to sleep for a hundred years before anything happened, and it wasn't a hundred years yet, now was it?

Even Barnaby found this a difficult assertion to refute, and so comparative quiet reigned, during which I found the mounting uneasiness of the last few hours coming to a head.

Why hadn't Richard come home at the time expected? Why hadn't he phoned? How come he hadn't even arrived at his office this morning? Why — and this, of course, was the huge, dark question looming over my meditations — why had his mysterious disappearance coincided so exactly with Edwin's allegedly unpremeditated visit to the Barlows' home?

Coincidence? Don't be silly! You *know* there must be a connection.

But a sinister one? Quite unbidden, and indeed in defiance of common sense, a picture flashed into my mind of Richard's body half-hidden among the tall dusty nettles and the dangling autumnal curtains of traveller's joy which must surely line the margins of that footpath at the far end of the garden. In my vision, blood was soaking into Richard's white shirt (did Richard wear white shirts? I couldn't remember from our one and only meeting, but anyway, that's how it indelibly was in my imagination) and blood had dried on his jacket. His face I couldn't visualise, never having seen a dead person (such sheltered lives we lead, amid the slaughter and mayhem of our TV screens). Nor could I visualise the wound from which the blood was flowing — never having seen a wound either — nor imagine with what kind of a weapon it could have been inflicted. A penknife? Well, yes, Edwin possessed a penknife, but would that be adequate for the scenario which my imagination was conjuring up? Had he, then, slipped our breadknife? — carving knife? — into his briefcase before hurrying — so swiftly, so furtively, a bag of nerves if ever there was one — out of our house this morning?

What would be the next scene in the drama?

The TV screen, of course. We would be sitting, Edwin and I, side by side, safely home just in time for the six o'clock news, on which the murder of the distinguished journalist Richard Barlow would take pride of place. Sidelong, I would be glancing at Edwin's face: sidelong, he would be glancing at mine; a penny for your thoughts . . . No, no, a penny would not be the appropriate coin at all, at all . . .

Sally was laughing at something Edwin had just said, and I was brought back to reality with a jolt . . . Lying back, eyes half closed, sunbathing in the last of the autumn sunshine, Edwin presented a persona impossible to slot into the role allotted by my fevered imagination. So laid-back he looked, so contented, so — I have to say it — so *trivial* a person; he just couldn't be the perpetrator of huge crimes, any more than he had been capable of huge deeds of daring. Angry, frightened, caught in a very tight corner indeed as a result of his own lies and deceptions, he might well have fantasized Richard's death;

106

might even have devised wild, imaginary plans for bringing it about: but when it came to the point — Ah, no! Not my Edwin!

And, after all, was there not another, and perfectly innocuous explanation for Richard's sudden disappearance today? Quite possibly, he had caught sight of Edwin lurking around the neighbourhood this morning — as by Sally's account he had undoubtedly been doing — and had resolved to get the hell out of the house before some sort of embarrassing encounter was forced upon him.

Of course! What could be more understandable?

All the same, this didn't explain why Edwin had come here so furtively, so unannounced in the first place. If not to murder Richard, then to do what to him?

To threaten? To plead? To bargain? And then, finding the bird flown, and himself irretrievably spotted lurking on the footpath, he had done the only sensible thing — had turned the whole thing into a casual social call. And a singularly pleasant one, as things turned out. And why not? Such innocent fun as it all was, the two of them basking idly in the sunshine under a dazzlingly blue sky framed by the massed loops and curves of multi-coloured autumn foliage.

"Daddy! Daddy!"

Barnaby's shriek of welcome was the first indication to any of us that Richard was home again, safe and sound, making his way swiftly across the lawn towards us. Sally and Edwin, sprawled side by side on the rug, both lurched to a sitting position far more guiltily than the actual situation warranted; Edwin, in particular, looked as if he had seen a ghost.

For a few seconds we were all struck motionless, as in a game of Grandmother's Footsteps, while Richard, despite his slight limp, came on apace, albeit encumbered by the clutching, squealing Barnaby.

107

CHAPTER XVI

We drove home almost in silence, Edwin and I. My mind was in a turmoil of suspicion, panic, and an overwhelming reluctance to confront Edwin about anything at all. Not now, anyway. Maybe the perfect time would be presently? It often is.

And Edwin's mind? In a turmoil too, I have no doubt, but the actual ingredients of that turmoil I could only guess at.

That moment of confrontation with Richard on the Barlow's lawn had not, after all, resulted in a stand-up row. Richard had behaved impeccably. In accordance with his creed, the host-to-guest relationship was given absolute precedence over the victim-to-murderer one (if that indeed was how he already saw it?). He greeted me and Edwin with polite correctness and with no sign of surprise at our presence, and he endorsed without flinching his wife's eager suggestion that we should stay for tea.

The tea-time conversation centred, naturally, on Richard's day-long absence. There had been a problem with the car, he said, he had needed the help of the AA to get it to a garage. From there, he had phoned the office explaining his delay, and asking them to ring his home to say he wouldn't be back for lunch . . .

"And they didn't, of course," broke in Sally. "It's that new girl of yours, darling, that June Somebody, she's always forgetting things and muddling messages. And you can't wonder, because do you know what her boyfriend said when he broke it off with her . . .? I mean, if you *have* to break it off with someone, you can at least . . ."

"Darling! The things you know!"

Instead of being irritated by the foolish irrelevance of the interruption, Richard was beaming round at us all.

"Sally's marvellous! *Everyone* confides in her about *everything*! She knows more about the girls in our office after a two-minute telephone conversation than I've learned in ten years of daily contact! Don't you, darling?"

His eyes feasted on her as she giggled her appreciation, her bright hair falling across her face as she relaxed yet more deeply into the armchair in which she was curled.

We were having tea in the drawing-room, the sudden chill of the autumn evening having swept in icy shadows across the lawn and driven us indoors. Daphne was pouring tea into delicate china cups — Rockingham china, I think — and she had paused when Sally began speaking. Unlike her son, she had been irritated, I could tell, by the girl's irrelevant interruption, but was making a more or less successful effort not to show it.

"Well, never mind," she said now, "*You* were all right, Richard, that's the main thing. But what was wrong with the car? It was serviced only a month or so ago, wasn't it?"

Richard shrugged.

"I know. Most annoying. I must have a word with them at our own garage. It was the brakes, actually: most remiss of whoever was responsible; there could have been a nasty accident. When I think how it might have happened when *Sally* was driving, fetching Barnaby from the nursery, or something . . . I feel quite sick . . ."

Discussion of the brakes followed. What could have caused such a sudden failure? How could it have escaped notice earlier?

"They'll be able to tell me more tomorrow," said Richard. "At a first glance, the chap said, it looked as if they'd been tampered with, but . . ."

"Those boys!" broke in Sally. "That wretched gang who went round stealing petrol caps last summer . . . you remember? Just for the hell of it — they couldn't possibly have had any *use* for them!"

"Those were cars left out in the road," pointed out Daphne. "Since we always put our car away in the garage, I don't see how anyone could have . . ."

"But the garage doors weren't locked," here broke in Edwin. "A gang of boys could easily have . . ."

The sudden stillness must have made him realise what he was saying; with clumsy haste he struggled to get out of it.

"I mean," he stumbled on, "one doesn't always lock one's garage doors, does one? Not if one's in a hurry, I mean . . . if one is going out again very shortly. Or one can forget . . ."

"So one can," observed Richard drily. "One is capable, it seems, of all sorts of things, isn't one?"

Here Sally rushed in to save the situation — though whether, at this stage, she realised there was a situation to be saved, I shall never know. "It was *me*, Richard darling! It was my fault, I'm terribly dreadfully sorry. *I* left the doors unlocked! After I'd brought Barnaby back from the play-group yesterday, I thought I'd be going out again straight after lunch, you see, it was my aerobics afternoon, but then Maisie rang up to say it was cancelled because of Gwen's husband having to go into hospital. He's had this trouble with his sinuses, you see, and they were going to do tests, but they'd had to put the appointment forward, and so . . ."

"And so my naughty little Sally didn't lock the garage doors!" said Richard, smiling, shaking his head. "Really, darling, you *should* be more careful . . ."

But no, she shouldn't, his look said. He loved her to be like that, despite inconveniences such as fatal accidents due to faulty brakes.

"My wife leads a charmed life," he smiled. "Whatever silly thing she does, it always works out all right in the end. Like now, for instance. Here I am, alive and well, am I not, in the teeth of all the disastrous possibilities? She's like that — her charmed life extends to everyone in contact with her. It's amazing! In spite of which, do, please, darling, lock the garage in future? Even if the aerobics class *isn't* cancelled. OK?"

Very OK, evidently. Sally, overwhelmed with sheer happiness at having so effortlessly delighted her husband with her carelessness, promised faithfully that she would be more careful in future, indeed she would: while Daphne, lips firmly and diplomatically closed, poured second cups of tea for us all.

Soon after this we left, Edwin and I, Richard playing the perfect host to the very end, even to the extent of expressing the hope that we might meet again before long.

On a seventeenth-century duelling-ground, with pistols? Or where? I shuddered when I thought about who it was who would inevitably lose.

And so we embarked on our silent drive home.

How much did Edwin know that I knew? That I suspected, rather — I mustn't let myself admit that I *knew* anything.

Though of course I did: and before the evening was over, I was to know more.

CHAPTER XVII

I wonder how many marriages have been saved — or at least had their break-up postponed — by television? Not many, you may say, if you go by the divorce statistics: but who knows how much worse these figures might be *without* these structured respites from one-to-one communication? The relief to me and Edwin of being able to switch on a programme about the balance of payments deficit the moment we walked into the house was indescribable: from that moment on, neither of us had to say *anything*.

I know the experts tell us that the stepping-up of communication between the partners is the prime recipe for improving a bad marriage: I'm sorry, but it's a lie. As a way of enriching yet further an already happy marriage — maybe: but as a recipe for saving an unhappy one it's a total non-starter, for in nine cases out of ten it's communication that has got them into this trouble in the first place. If only she hadn't told him that she found Shakespeare boring, then maybe he would never have been alerted to the other symptoms of her execrable taste: the flight of pottery ducks across the bedroom wall and the appearance of tomato ketchup on the table at every meal might well have passed unnoticed. And if only he'd never confided to her that he was sick to death of hearing about starving children on the radio, then it is probable that she would never have started on that dossier of non-compassionate remarks uttered by him, and from which she can quote with such good effect whenever he refuses to do something that she wants done.

The truth is that unhappy marriages come about in large measure as the end result of a prolonged exercise in communication: in particular, the communicating of unflattering truths on a wide variety of topics, ranging from the correct handling of a tube of toothpaste to the squandering of the family fortunes on drink or self-awareness courses. In these sort of cases, 'Least Said Soonest Mended' would be my proverb of choice. Certainly it has long seemed to be the right proverb for me and Edwin: provided we kept off sensitive subjects, such as almost everything, we have been able to rub along pretty well for a lot of the time.

Of course, in the last few days our no-go areas of conversation had increased dramatically. On top of all the usual taboo subjects, we now couldn't talk about editors, garages, journeys across London, phases of the moon, newspaper headlines or tomato soup flavoured with fennel. Even the weather was tricky, reminiscent as it might be of the sunlit afternoon on the Barlows' lawn.

So, the balance of payments deficit was exactly right. We had never quarrelled about the balance of payments deficit, Edwin and I; it was a genuinely neutral subject between us, and so for nearly an hour we were able to sit side by side, not listening, but enjoying something really rather like peace — there is no other word for it. We were relieved not only from the need to say anything, but also from the stress and strain of not speaking to each other. What couples did before there was television, I can't imagine. There were books, of course, but the trouble with these is that to sit separately, each with a good book, carries an aura of not-speaking which watching TV in silence doesn't. I suppose it's because *somebody* is speaking, even though it's not you.

The balance of payments crisis was succeeded by a fairly pretty girl giving lightening answers to lightening questions about the life and works of Archbishop Laud — again a subject on which

Edwin and I had mercifully never differed; and before this was over, there came the first of the evening's telephone calls.

Even though Edwin's brief burst of fame seemed to be at an end, there were still quite a lot of callers: friends, acquaintances, relatives seeking to congratulate or to ask questions; not to mention the increasingly fed-up editor of *International Focus*, contact with whom Edwin was still sedulously avoiding.

Partly because of this, and partly because I felt that I could more plausibly fail to answer the man's questions than could Edwin himself, I made a point of being the one to get to the phone first each time it rang (not that there was any perceptible competition); and thus it came about that it was I (mercifully) who was the one to get the brunt of Jason's indignation. He was ringing, I gathered, from the home of his friend Tim:

"Look, Mum, I've been trying to get you for ages! What have you done with my boletus?"

Boletus? Boletus? Then the penny dropped.

"My dear Jason, I haven't done anything! I — "

Then I remembered. Of course: last night I'd shoved the thing hastily behind the breadbin so that Edwin wouldn't catch sight of it and make some kind of a fuss: but of course I couldn't explain this to Jason. For years now, I had been fighting a losing battle to kid Jason that he had a steady, fair-minded father who could be counted on to judge things rationally; and though it hadn't worked — not for the last decade at least — it still seemed better than open treachery. I think Jason felt it to be better, too — anyway, he played along, so long as the issue wasn't one really important to him. This one, apparently, was, and so I must choose my words carefully.

"I'm sorry, Jason," I said, "I was giving the kitchen a good clear up, and I put it on the dresser. Behind the breadbin. I meant to tell you, but you'd already gone off to school. And anyway, I thought you'd taken it. It was gone by the time I got up."

114

"No, of course I didn't take it, that's why I'm ringing! And it *wasn't* behind the breadbin; I looked everywhere. It's a bit rotten, you know, because I promised Tim — I *told* you I wanted to show it to him, because according to his book . . ."

I'm sorry. Sorry, sorry, sorry. What else could I be? I hadn't got the thing, hadn't thrown it away, well, of course I hadn't, what an idea!

All the same, it did seem to be vaguely my fault. This is an attitude, I know, which Women's Lib have been fighting against for years, this guilt-complex of the typical housewife: her feeling that everything that goes wrong in the home is *her* fault.

Well, I agree with them in deploring this attitude, especially when I catch myself succumbing to it: the only thing I'd say is that it isn't basically a guilt-complex at all, it's more to do with power. If everything is your fault, then it stands to reason that everything was under your control in the first place: and what is this but megalomania on the grand scale? It seems clear that much of what masquerades as guilt is merely a power-crazy delusion; an arrogant assumption of personal power ludicrously at variance with the reality.

If the situation in which Jason and I found ourselves at this juncture had been less acerbic, I might have put this theory to him, and we could have had an interesting discussion; but this was clearly not the moment. And so the call petered out unsatisfactorily, with me saying that if it turned up I'd ring him at Tim's, and him saying that that would be too late, as they were both going out as soon as they had finished supper: at which meal, presumably, the errant fungus was to have featured in all its glory, fried in butter. Oh, well, it can't be helped: we rang off, in a mood of mutual dissatisfaction.

The next two calls were easier: one from my old schoolfriend Gladys, saying how lovely it must be for me to have Edwin home again, and me saying, Yes, wasn't it: and the second from my temping agency, saying they'd got a job for me tomorrow afternoon, and probably for the rest of the week as someone had just let them down, and so . . .

I accepted, though very uneasily. I had already turned down two offers since Edwin's return, on the grounds of having too much on my plate at home; I couldn't go on doing this for ever, though the temptation continued to be great. This is the trouble with temping: it sounds marvellous, this option of working or not working as one's life-situation permits, giving yourself a break whenever there's something to worry about at home; but it's a snare really because, actually, there's always something to worry about at home. *This* week, that is: *next* week will be clear. Until it arrives, that is, at which point it inevitably becomes *this* week, and we start all over again . . .

Still, as I say, you can't go on turning jobs down for ever, and so, "Yes", I said; and Edwin, hovering a few feet away — eavesdropping, one might say — wanted to know what I was saying 'Yes' to? He seemed to be really agitated, and I tried to guess what he might be imagining I was assenting to . . . but before anything had been resolved, the phone went yet again.

"Yes?" I said. "Yes, this is Mrs Wakefield speaking," and waited. The South Dulwich Botanical Research Centre, the cultured voice explained. "Your husband was here this morning with a rather interesting specimen of fungus which he urgently wanted identified. I just wanted to let him know that it's non-poisonous, perfectly edible. It *is* a boletus, tell him, though an exceptionally large one. The unusual purplish tinge is simply due to . . ."

"Edwin," I said, "this is for you," and I thrust the receiver at him as if it had bitten me. I didn't want to hear any more, and to make sure that I didn't I headed swiftly for the kitchen, slamming the door behind me.

CHAPTER XVIII

With the morning came a letter for me, handwritten, with a Norfolk postmark. By extreme ill-luck, Edwin had been the one right there in the hall as the letter came through the box, and he was now standing over me, like a terrier at a rabbit-hole, watching for me to open it.

I don't know what good I thought my delaying tactics would do, they were instinctive really. Slowly, I spread another blob of marmalade on my last scrap of toast. Languidly, and with extreme reluctance, I started on the junk mail, actually reading it for the first time ever. A £25,000 car was to be mine: 'You have drawn one of the lucky numbers, Mrs Wakefield, which entitles you to take part in our Grand something-something . . .' I could feel Edwin's impatience gathering around the back of my neck and down my shoulder blades.

He wasn't going to go away. No sense in prolonging the agony. Like a suicide nerving himself for the final leap, I drew a deep breath, reached for a knife, and slit open the fatal missive.

Well, not fatal exactly. Indeed, on the face of it, it was *good* news. Leonard Coburn had been pronounced well enough to be flown home within the next few days, and the next half-page of Jessica's letter was filled with expressions of wifely relief and rapture.

BUT . . . and there followed a fairly extensive list of all the problems, difficulties and inconveniences attendant on this rapturous event at just this exact moment in Jessica's life. How, for instance, was she to meet him at the airport now she was on this anti-histamine drug which meant that she couldn't drive? And then — wasn't it just her luck?! — her daily woman had gone sick, and so how in the world was she going to cope with an invalid as well as all the housework.

"And it's such a *big* house, you know, and really dreadfully inconvenient, but of course Leo loves it . . ."

And so on and so on. Did it all add up to a request for me to go and help out in some way . . . ? Before I had reached the end of the six closely written pages, Edwin had burst out with his own answer:

"The poor woman! We must drive up and help her *at once*! We can't leave her in all this trouble . . . We must start *now*!"

I don't know if he thought that this unprecedented burst of altruism was actually going to deceive me? Or did he know very well — and gamble on it making no difference — that I knew exactly what his real motive was? Clearly, he wanted to be there, on the spot, to prevent any disastrous reunion between Leonard and Richard; already he could envisage them backing up one another's accounts of the expedition, and giving the lie to him, Edwin, so decisively that no amount of twisting and pre-varicating on his part could possibly extricate him.

As before, my first instinct was to delay things.

"But Edwin — we can't possibly — not just like that — right now. What about Jason . . . ?"

I had brought it on myself, I admit it. The angry explosion about fifteen-year-olds being to all intents and purposes adults, who could surely be left to run their own lives for a day or two without all this ridiculous nannying?

There have been other occasions, of course, when the opposite theme has ricocheted off our walls, about how fifteen-year-olds are still irresponsible children who shouldn't be allowed out in the evenings without saying exactly where they were going and being back by nine.

I kept my head down, as I usually did when this fraught subject

118

got its periodic airing, and waited for the steam to go out of it. Which it did, of course, after a few minutes, and Edwin, unable to think of anything more to say, slammed out of the kitchen.

Slowly, my mind a whirl of plans and counter-plans, I carried the breakfast crockery to the sink, put away the marmalade, the milk, the butter, and found myself calculating, as I contemplated the contents of the refrigerator, what I could leave for Jason's meal tonight . . . whether there was enough milk . . . cheese . . . orange juice to tide him over?

So had I already decided we must go to Norfolk today? In spite of knowing Edwin's real motive for wishing to do so? The decision — if it was a decision — shocked me, and I wondered where it had come from? Only a few days ago, sitting on that damp dead log in the damp autumnal wood, I had been wrestling — or thought I had been wrestling — with the original decision about whether to back Edwin up in his deception — as perhaps a loyal wife should? — or whether (in his long-term interest, perhaps?) — to expose him as the liar that he was — or at least to use whatever influence I had to force him to a public confession?

I had no sense of having succeeded in coming to any decision about this tangled moral dilemma; and yet now, after only three days, I found that the decision had in fact been irrevocably made: not by any clear act of will on my part, but by a series of small, *ad hoc* evasions; moments of taking the line of least resistance; of not interrupting him when his discourse took off into flights of fancy; of taking a non-controversial stance on every issue as it cropped up. By all these escapist manoeuvres I found myself, now, committed inescapably to helping him save face; to protecting him from himself by heading him off from whatever wild and desperate schemes might be churning inside his panicky soul. First and foremost, to head him off from trying to murder Richard, which, it was clear by now, he had already attempted more than once — though with such monumental inefficiency that one could not help wondering how realistic the intention had actually been? Anyway, the risk was there, and I was the only

119

person in the world who was in a position to monitor Edwin's movements, to make sure that the opportunity for murder never arose.

And now there was Leonard Coburn, too. Once back in England, he too would be at risk. All this frantic urgency to set off this very day to go and 'help' in the Coburns' Norfolk home seemed to me sinister in the extreme. Clearly, Edwin was determined to be first on the spot when Leonard arrived home, and somehow to prevent him making contact with Richard.

Somehow? How? I found my hands trembling as I put away the glasses, each one clinking a tiny, horrid little message to me about the state of my nerves.

I must calm down . . . calm down. No good would come of my allowing myself to become just as hysterical as Edwin himself . . .

It was as this thought went through my mind that it occurred to me that Edwin had been extraordinarily quiet during these last few minutes. I would have expected him, in the course of packing for this headlong trip, to have been in and out of the kitchen half a dozen times, howling for clean socks, for ironed handkerchiefs, for the one and only shirt which happened, at just this moment, to be the one which hadn't been washed. Racing up and down the stairs, too, searching here there and everywhere for reading glasses, distance glasses, clip-on sunglasses, road map, bankcard, the lot. All the things which any wife other than me would have been able to lay her hands on unerringly, and without a moment's hesitation.

Well, the clip-on sunglasses I *could* help him with. And he would need them, too, driving in an easterly direction this early in the day. They were right here, inside the soup tureen which, long since missing a lid, had become the receptacle of choice for just this sort of thing — objects that are wanted desperately, and with extreme urgency, but only now and then.

"Edwin," I called, opening the door into the hall, "your sunglasses . . ."

Silence. Out I went into the hall, to the foot of the stairs.

"Edwin!" I shouted.

Still no answer. Seized by sudden apprehension, I ran into the sitting-room and looked out of the window.

Yes, the car was gone. Without a word to me, he had sneaked off, making no pre-journey fuss about anything, in total silence, shutting the front door furtively behind him.

My first instinct was to follow him, immediately. To ring up a taxi, to head for Liverpool Street, and jump on to the first train to King's Lynn whence there would be some sort of connection (surely there would) to Dereham Market.

But why? What was the rush? Leonard Coburn wouldn't be home yet. 'The end of the week', Jessica had said in her letter, and today was only Tuesday. Until Leonard actually arrived, surely there was nothing in the way of mischief that Edwin could get up to?

I must reread Jessica's letter, and see exactly what she *had* said: but — wouldn't you know it? — the letter was gone. Edwin must have decided he wanted it with him, either to pore over at leisure and without interference by me, or else as a sort of passport to legitimise his sudden and unannounced descent on his possibly reluctant hostess. "But look, you *asked* us to come, " he could say, and he would point to the bit of the letter which perhaps could — just — be interpreted that way.

I sat down at the kitchen table and collected my thoughts. There *wasn't* all that much hurry, there really wasn't. I needn't, after all, cancel my temping job yet again. It would be finished by six, I could be home in time to get Jason's supper and explain to him — with suitable omissions — what we were doing, and still be able to get a train from Liverpool Street.

By rights, I should at this point have rung Jessica Coburn to find out what kind of help, if any, she was asking for: but then what was I going to do if it turned out to be something I could perfectly well do for her here in London? I *had* to go, now that Edwin had gone, whether she wanted me or not; and so what would be the point of finding out that she didn't?

CHAPTER XIX

King's Lynn in time for the connection to Dereham Halt. Well, that's how it was going to be in theory, that is, in the small print of the Eastern Region Winter Timetable. But I was reckoning without the idiosyncrasies of today's transport systems. It was nearly midnight when the train, after many a pause for thought, arrived at King's Lynn, and I disembarked on to a brightly lit but totally deserted platform. No one in the booking office, no one behind any of the doors marked 'Private', and nothing written up on the indicator board. In spite of the brilliant illumination elsewhere, the waiting-room was in darkness. Still, at least it was open, and I could feel grateful that whoever had forgotten to put a bulb in the light socket had also forgotten to lock the door when he went off duty. So there was somewhere to sit sheltered from the wind, though of course one couldn't read one's book in there. For that, one had to stand on the bright, freezing platform buffeted by the east wind. One was spoilt for choice.

Twenty to one. Presumably there would be *some* sort of a train, some time? A freight train, perhaps? Nuclear waste, or something? Every now and then I would start up from my uneasy doze in the dark waiting-room, fancying I heard a singing of the rails, heralding the approach of a train, but always it was nothing, just the gusts of wind, rising and falling. And then I would stay outside for a little, trying to read, until the wicked cold drove me in again, to sit on the hard bench, shivering and half-dozing in the darkness.

123

And so, sitting, standing, cowering, shivering, I edged and pushed myself through the recalcitrant stretches of the night until at last, icy cold and almost believing that time itself had come to a stop, I saw, with incredulous joy, that another living being, hunched in a greatcoat had come on to the platform; and then another, and another. It was five-fifteen. The workmen's train was due at last.

By six o'clock I had reached my destination — or, rather, the windswept local station about three miles, so far as I could judge from my map, from the Coburn's home. It was still dark, and I felt it to be far too early to be bothering a prospective hostess — especially one who has been more or less press ganged into the role — and so I decided not to set off along the road straight away, but to walk down to the sea. I could tell the direction by the fierce, salty wind that hit me as I stepped out into the station forecourt.

The darkness was lifting now, just a little, and I was able to make my way down a rutted track which led, after about a quarter of a mile, to a wild, windswept landscape of sand dunes and marram grass, the stiff, wintry blades rattling and rustling under the gusts of the dawn wind.

Stumbling and slithering, clutching my suitcase, I clambered to the top of the first dune, and there — Oh, the sudden sense of being on a planet, hurtling through space, overwhelmed me. Dwarfed and battered by the gigantic and random forces of Earth's atmosphere, I struggled to get my breath; then turned to face the huge curve of the sea, beyond which the first silvery streaks of dawn were breaking, flicking into sharp relief the long white rims of the waves that moaned across the sand towards me.

There must have been a storm during the night, and for a moment I felt a slight sense of shock as I saw, a mile or so further along the coast, the outlines of a sunken ship. Was I the sole witness of a maritime disaster? Should I do something? Fetch somebody? But before I had come to any sort of decision, the light had already brightened, and I could see now that this was

124

indeed a wreck, but a very long-ago one. With its broken rails and rotting uptilted bows, it had probably been lying there half-submerged for years.

The sky low in the east was becoming yellow now, a pale lemon yellow and then pink; flashes of pink radiance danced across the tumbled waters and touched the stretches of wet sand with streaks of light. One could imagine slithering down the sand dune, down and down to that expanse of shining sand, on and on to the curved edge of the water and beyond, to share totally in the burgeoning of the new day as the planet tipped one eastward towards the sun . . .

A numbness was stealing over me, I was stiff with cold; the wind chiselled past my ears, and what about my suitcase?

Welcome or not, too early or not, I must be on my way.

Once off the sand dunes and on the coast road, I began to feel less numb, more in charge of what I should do next. I didn't *have* to go straight to the Coburns'. There was the village, wasn't there, Dereham Market, where there might quite easily be some sort of café open serving breakfasts for building-site workers and farm labourers and so forth? I could sit there spinning out some sort of a meal and a cup of coffee for as long as I judged expedient.

By now, it was nearly full daylight, and I paused to study my map. It seemed that, from here, the village was on the *other* side of the Coburns' farm house; in fact I would have to go right past their gate to reach it, unless I made a deliberate detour. Oh, well, never mind. It would all help to fill in time.

The coast road, at this hour in the morning, was completely deserted. On one side the sand dunes cut off sight of the sea, but on the other barley fields — well I think it was barley, but of course at this time of year there was only stubble to be seen — stretched flat and bare to the other horizon, almost like a second sea.

I met no one, heard no sounds except for the endless whistling of the wind and the muffled thudding of the incoming tide beyond the dunes. There seemed to be no sign of human life anywhere, so I was quite startled when just round a bend in the road I came upon a parked car. It was parked half on the road, half on the sandy verge,

125

its front wheels partially sunk in the loose, powdery sand. I was even more startled when I took in that it was *our* car.

I read the number twice before I could believe it, and even then had to walk right up to it and peer in through the window in order to be convinced by the familiar clutter on the back seat. A torn rain-hat. Road maps too out of date to be any use, only we didn't want them indoors either. A thermos flask with its cap missing so that nothing stays hot in it. And, in the back, Edwin's tennis racket dating from the days before he quarrelled with the secretary of our local tennis club — I forget what about, and actually I think it was more that Edwin was putting on weight and losing his knack; but anyway, there the tennis racket has remained. Well, we didn't want that indoors either. I didn't, anyway: it would only end up as one more thing in the kitchen, leaning against something.

I tried the doors, but of course they were locked, and so, I just stood there, trying, weakly, to make sense of the situation. That Edwin had driven up yesterday of course I knew — but why leave the car *here*? Why not have driven right to the house, and parked in the Coburns' front yard, or wherever?

Had he, for some devious reason of his own, not wanted Jessica to know that he had come by car? Why not? Did he want to avoid having to drive her to the airport to meet her husband when the time came? This, actually, was the one and only obvious bit of help he could have given her. To have come all this way more or less uninvited, and then refuse to give her this bit of help, would be intolerably ungracious even by Edwin's standards. And anyway, why? Surely, the whole motive for this trip was to make contact with Leonard as soon as he possibly could, before Richard had a chance to do so? This must be his motive, surely? Nothing else made sense. What, exactly, he had in mind to do, having made this contact, I hadn't yet begun to speculate. I think I was avoiding doing so. I didn't want to know what he was planning, I only knew that I must be on hand to frustrate it. How, I didn't know. Simply by being there presumably, and keeping an eye on everything all of the time.

I tried the doors again, and also the boot. All locked. It then occurred to me — a most simple and obvious explanation — that Edwin might genuinely have run into trouble with the vehicle? Just because someone is planning a murder, it doesn't follow that they are no longer subject to the ordinary hazards of life — flat batteries, leaking oil and so forth. Murderers can catch flu, suffer nosebleeds and lose their reading glasses just as easily as anyone else; it just *seems* incongruous somehow.

So, if I waited around, Edwin might turn up, complete with plausible explanation.

Did I want him to turn up?

Did I want to hear the explanation?

I did not. I continued on my way.

It wasn't until I was sitting at a plastic-topped table in a small, fairly grimy café in Dereham Market, with a cup of coffee and a rock bun in front of me, that an idea came into my head which was more disturbing than anything I had yet thought of. Supposing Edwin, defeated at last by the evermore complex web of deceit he had been weaving around himself, had decided to end it all? There at hand was the grey, sounding sea, not a soul in sight from horizon to horizon, no witnesses, no would-be rescuers — would he be tempted, even momentarily, to take the easy way out?

If it *had* been easy, then maybe, yes. But of course it wouldn't be. Edwin was a strong swimmer — or had been; maybe a bit out of training now, but still pretty good — and surely no one even half-competent in the water is going to choose death by drowning? For a swimmer, it cannot be an easy death; on the contrary, he will face hours and hours of mounting exhaustion, and yet still be debarred from succumbing to it, for all the time you *can* swim just one more stroke, however agonising, your body will force you to do so . . .

No. Not Edwin. Not anybody really. I tried to picture Edwin facing even the earliest stage of this ordeal . . . the first steps into the icy water . . . the freezing ache mounting to his knees . . .

127

his thighs . . . the wind slicing past his bare torso, and unable, this time, to say to himself "I'll just dip in for a moment, and then dash out". For there would be no dashing out, ever again. Once in, he would have to stay there. For ever.

No. Not Edwin.

All the same, I hastily finished the rock bun, swallowed half the coffee, and hurried out into the narrow street.

By now, it was bright morning, the blue, windswept sky dazzling above the bare, brown fields, and the sun hot on my shoulders as I walked, or rather half-ran, along the field path which the café proprietor had pointed out to me as the quickest way to Coburn's Farm. I could see the grey building, foursquare to the winds, ahead of me, with its barns and outbuildings: and the nearer I came, the more I was aware of my heart thudding behind my ribs.

Of course, I'd been running. Or more or less running.

I pulled the massive dangling chunk of iron that looked as if it operated a bell, and sure enough it did. I heard the hollow peal clanging round and round the unseen stone spaces within, and it sounded to my jangled nerves like the Trump of Doom. What was I going to find? With what news would I be greeted?

The door was opened, warily — or was it merely very heavy? — by a very young girl who looked about fourteen, with a round freckled face and a mouth slightly open. Without a word she led me across the stone-flagged hall, pushed open another heavy door, and stood, clutching it, while I made my entrance.

Surprise, quite as much as relief, stopped me in my tracks. There, sitting round a bright log fire, drinking coffee, sat three people: Edwin, his hostess and a stout lady I did not know. Animated conversation had been going on, and when they turned at my entrance, with varying degrees of welcome, the tail end of a smile was fading from each face. They'd been having fun, and I'd interrupted it.

CHAPTER XX

I had assumed (a recognised sympton of anxiety, this) that they'd
been talking about me, but of course they hadn't. After the brief
flurry attendant on my arrival, I found myself with a cup of good
hot coffee in my hand, the welcome warmth from the flames
playing on my legs and listening to the plump lady (a Mrs
Fairbrother, I learned, from the other side of the village) holding
forth on the subject of werewolves. Apparently a film crew had
recently been on location in the marshes alongside the estuary,
setting up backgrounds for a new horror film on the subject, and
they'd got it all wrong.

"For a start, a marsh is entirely the wrong setting," Rhoda
Fairbrother was declaring. "The werewolf legend belongs to
forests, but some people seem to have got the idea that 'Were' is
an old word for 'Marsh' — mixing it up with 'Mere' perhaps? But
of course it isn't, it's just the word for 'Man' in Old Dutch —
'Man-Wolf' . . .

"My goodness, you *have* been doing your homework!"
interposed Jessica, with just that touch of jocular reprimand with
which a hostess tries to indicate to Guest A that his pet subject is
about to become boring to Guests B, C, and D. "Have another
biscuit?"

"Oh — I mean, thank you, no, I still have one," Rhoda
Fairbrother hastily quelled the interruption, waving her custard-
cream in the air impatiently: then continued:

"So absolutely wrong they've got it — really, you'd think

they'd got it mixed up with the Hound of the Baskervilles! You know, this monstrous dog looming up through the mist and baying across the marshes. But the whole point of a werewolf is that by day he isn't a monster at all. By day, he is a man, a perfectly ordinary man, unless you happen to know the signs. Eyebrows meeting in the middle is one of the wolf-marks. Another is secret indulgence in cannibalism. The eating of children, you know, was rife right across Europe during the famines of the seventh and eighth centuries . . ."

Throughout this dissertation, I had been watching Edwin's face. Far from being bored, he had the air of a student picking up last-minute tips for a forthcoming examination. I think Jessica must have noticed the intensity of his interest, for she quickly gave up her hostessy little interventions, and allowed her knowledgeable guest a free rein. As a keen local historian, Rhoda was understandably enjoying her role as expert putting in its place a brash American film crew bent on piling up box office horrors rather than on getting anything right.

"Though of course," she conceded, "a certain amount of confusion is understandable, because over the centuries there have been many werewolf legends. The most widespread is that the man actually and physically turns into a wolf at night, so that if the wolf should be wounded, then the man next morning will display the corresponding injuries. Another belief is that he simply projects his soul into a real wolf, and from inside its brain directs it to do terrible things. According to some historians, the whole thing may have been drug-induced, a sort of mass-hallucination on the part of both the populace and the alleged werewolf — he fantasizing that he really is a wolf, and going lolloping around on all fours, biting and foaming at the mouth; and the populace hallucinating a real wolf as he charges among them inflicting terrible injuries . . ."

"Hallucinating?" Edwin pounced on the word like a cat on a half-fledged bird. "Drug-induced, didn't you say? *What* drug?"

Rhoda beamed with pleasure, and smoothed back her grey-

130

blonde curls. It wasn't often, I felt sure, that she encountered such an assiduous imbiber of her historical expertise.

"Now, that's a *very* interesting question. There are any number of theories, but the one that I personally find the most convincing is that it was ergot. As you may know (clearly she imagined, poor soul, that she had found a fellow-enthusiast for medieval history) the harvests in Europe during the eleventh and twelfth centuries were catastrophic. It was the time of the little ice-age, and a series of wet, cold summers meant that most crops were affected by blight, producing the poison ergot. Contemporary evidence suggests that many people knew that their grain was poisonous — but what could they do? They were starving. Of course, they ate it, and they suffered accordingly. Hallucinations were a major sympton, but not the only one by any means . . ."

"What were the others?" Edwin was leaning forward, alert and attentive, for all the world as if he were collecting data for some article. Only the notebook was missing, and the tape recorder, and the prospect of a fee.

"The others?" Rhoda was racking her well-stocked brain. "Well, fever of course. Headache. Mania sometimes. Mental confusion . . ."

"Amnesia?" here chipped in Edwin. "Could it cause amnesia?"

"Why — yes, I should think so. Anything like that. The whole brain would be to some extent deranged, you see, all the chemical messages haywire. I can't tell you the details, I'm not a pharmacist, you know. Just a *very* amateur historian."

"A very expert one, *I'd* say," remarked Edwin with warm approval; though what, exactly, he was approving of was anyone's guess. "I think it's all just fascinating."

There followed a tiny pause. Then: "This ergot stuff — what *is* it? I mean, is it *for* anything? As a chemical? Nowadays, I mean? Like, could you buy it at a chemist's?"

Sadly, Rhoda had to shake her head. Here was something she didn't know. Tragic.

131

But happily Jessica was able to fill the intellectual gap that threatened to yawn.

"Ergot? Oh, I can tell you all about ergot. It came into *Maternity Ward Three* on ITV. Did you see it? It's what they give to mothers after childbirth, to contract the womb, or something. Isn't that right?" She turned to me as to an authority, I being, apparently, the only person present who had had even one baby. In the country of the blind, the one-eyed man, etc . . .

But, alas, I hadn't had ergot when Jason was born. Or if I had, they didn't tell me. I hadn't had hallucinations, either. Altogether, I was a rather useless participant in the conversation.

"I think maybe it was before my time?" I ventured, casting my mind back to that bustling maternity ward; mothers in, mothers out, babies weighing more, less, or just the same as the next baby; never a dull minute. I remembered, too, Edwin striding towards my bed, grinning hugely, and bearing an absurdly gigantic bunch of gladioli, enough to upset both day and night staff at one go. How he had enjoyed the effortless glory of being a brand-new father! If only it could have remained both effortless and brand-new for ever!

By now, the conversation had moved on — or, perhaps one should say, back, for they were talking once again about amnesia. I had noticed how Edwin's face had fallen when he learned that ergot was a specific for childbirth, which put it hopelessly beyond the range of whatever it was he was plotting; but now, having manoeuvred the conversation back onto his chosen topic, he was holding forth in great style:

"By far the commonest cause of amnesia," he was explaining "is concussion. Upon recovering consciousness after a severe blow on the head, the patient often remembers nothing at all of the hours leading up to the injury. That is why it is notoriously difficult, in cases where assault is involved, or dangerous driving, to know how much credence to give to the patient's account of events . . .

132

'Notoriously difficult.' 'How much credence to give.' Edwin had been reading it up in some book, obviously. These weren't *his* phrases. I waited for the medical dissertation to continue, but at this point Jessica broke in:

"Yes, I've been worrying about that quite a bit. About Leo, I mean, when he gets back. I did ask Dr Davies about it, but he says not to worry, they wouldn't be letting him out of hospital if he'd still been having problems with the concussion. He's had a report from them already, and it seems that apart from his collar-bone, and his leg still in plaster, he's OK. In every other way he's in normal health — "

"*Normal?*" Again Edwin did his cat-pounce on a significant word. "In his general health — maybe. But his memory — that can't possibly be back to normal as soon as this. I don't want to frighten you, Jessica, and I'm sure he'll be just fine in every other way: it's just that those few hours of his life, just before the injury, will be blacked out completely. Or else distorted out of all recognition. It's always like that, and the important thing is not to let him worry about it. Just don't bring the subject up, that's the best thing."

Here he looked from one to another of us, and spoke with yet greater emphasis: "We must all be careful, when he gets home, not to ask him one single thing about the hours leading up to the attack. And if he himself starts talking about what he thinks he remembers, we must firmly discourage him. All of us. Is that understood?"

"Look, Edwin — " I began, but he flapped his hand to silence me.

"No, Clare, don't interrupt. What I'm saying is important. I've known no end of chaps in Leonard's situation, recovering from concussion, and if they're cross-questioned about what they remember, they can simply go round the bend, and start to hallucinate. They fancy they remember all sorts of things that didn't happen, and forget all sorts of things that did. They know that *something's* wrong, but they don't know what. It can be very

133

frightening for them, to be forced to confront their own delusions. I've seen it happen. I do know what I'm talking about."

He did, too. He'd been reading it up in a big way, and not just in our *Home Doctor's ABC*. He must have been scouring the libraries as well, and had picked out just those case histories which corresponded most closely to his requirements.

It's not difficult. Shut your eyes and think of something awful, and if you search through enough weighty medical tomes, you'll find an example of it.

You may ask — and indeed I have asked myself the same question many times — why I didn't challenge him the moment we found ourselves alone, and stop once and for all this dangerous lying? It would have been easy. All these chaps he had known recovering from concussion. Which chaps? When? On what occasion? I could have cornered him with the greatest of ease, and he must have known I could.

He trusted me not to, I'm not quite sure why. But in fact his trust — if that's what it was — was well-founded. I wasn't going to show him up because I didn't dare. This edifice of falsehood he was setting up as a bulwark against exposure and disgrace, it was a terrifyingly precarious structure, and growing more top-heavy day by day. If it collapsed, then what? To what desperate measures might he then resort?

For, in a way, the lies he had chosen to tell this morning had left me feeling slightly reassured. He was not, after all, planning to murder Leonard, but simply to rubbish his story in advance by all this talk of amnesia. It might work, it might not. Surely it would be wise to wait and see what actually happened before showing him up?

For one thing was certain: Edwin was a frightened man. By making a frightened man more frightened, you don't make him less dangerous: quite the reverse.

134

CHAPTER XXI

"I've put you in our room," Jessica was saying, showing me into a large, low-ceilinged room dominated by a huge four-poster bed, complete with cretonne curtains looped back against the ornately carved posts. Matching cretonne draped the lattice window through which the pale afternoon sunshine gleamed and leaped off polished oak; a dressing-table, a rocking chair, and a Victorian tallboy reaching almost to the beamed ceiling.

"You see, Leo's leg is going to be in plaster for some time yet, and so it'll be much easier for him to be downstairs. We've fixed up a spare bed in his study — Edwin helped Phoebe bring it downstairs, and the mattress too. Oh, Clare, he's been *such* a help, I can't tell you! I'm so glad I thought of writing to you — I almost didn't, you know, it seemed such cheek, but I was at my wits' end, and Edwin has been *so* reassuring. He says he'd never have forgiven me if I hadn't turned to him for help in this crisis, Leo being such a close friend, and a colleague and everything. And Leo will be thrilled to find him here, I know he will; they'll have so much to talk about after all they've been through together. And do you know, Clare, Edwin has even offered to type up Leo's reports for him, and cope with all the correspondence — Leo won't be able to type just yet, with his collar-bone and everything. He's our angel of mercy, your Edwin, he really is! And on top of all this, he's going to drive me to the airport when the time comes. I expect he told you, didn't he? Of course, the

135

car is in the garage at the moment, having the new wheel fixed, but it'll be ready in plenty of time, he says . . ."

"Whose car?" The Coburns' car? Or ours?

"Oh, yours, of course," said Jessica lightly. "Well naturally Edwin would be happier driving his own car, wouldn't he? Besides, I don't suppose he *could* drive ours anyway, all the fuss with third-party insurance and things. Anyway, it's going to be OK, they've promised it will be ready first thing in the morning, and Leo won't be arriving before Thursday or Friday at the earliest."

In a garage. A new wheel being fixed. The wheels had looked all right to me, and it certainly hadn't been in a garage.

Oh, well. What this latest bout of fibbing was in aid of I couldn't guess, but did I have to? The essential thing was for me to keep an eye on Edwin's every movement after Leo's arrival, starting by going with him and Jessica to the airport. On this I would have to insist. The possessive-wife image wasn't one which I relished: it would look as if I couldn't trust my husband alone in a car with the elegant Jessica and her shining pony-tail, whereas the truth was that I couldn't trust him anywhere, doing anything. But it couldn't be helped. In a crisis, one's self-image is often the first thing that has to go.

Jessica's relief at having us here was gratifyingly evident, though my role was not quite as clear as Edwin's. So far, all I had done was to wash up after lunch — not a very onerous task, the meal having consisted of corned beef, tomatoes, and sticks of celery. For the plainness of this meal Jessica had apologised fulsomely, despite our (mine, anyway) assurances that this was exactly the sort of lunch we had at home.

"It's all so difficult," she said, "my woman going sick at a time like this, it's most upsetting. Phoebe isn't the same at all. She's a nice enough girl and she means well, I daresay, but she's supposed to be still at school really; she won't be sixteen till the end of the month, and I have to show her *everything*! She doesn't even know that the small knife has to go *outside* the large knife when she's laying the table! I ask you! And she can't stay after four, because that's when her mother expects her home — her mother thinks she's been to school you see — and so I'm left with the whole evening on my hands. The evening meal. Feeding the geese. *Everything*!

"Look, Clare, I've cleared a drawer for you — here — " She pulled open the middle drawer of a bow-fronted chest of drawers. "I hope that'll be enough . . . I hope I've thought of everything . . ." Her eyes roved anxiously round the room, while I assured her as emphatically as I could that everything was absolutely fine, what a lovely room it was; I just love those old beams — and a real old-fashioned patchwork bedspread, too! — and what a gorgeous view!

As indeed it was. Moving beside me to the lattice window, Jessica raised the latch and pushed it open on to the wide, bare landscape of dunes and sea and sky. The salty air, already laced with the chill of evening, swept past us into the room, and I drew deep breaths of a larger, clearer world, away and beyond the turmoil of my present life. Whatever happened, whatever Edwin was plotting, was tiny compared with the vastness of this sky.

"It's the draughts that are the problem," Jessica was gently complaining. "It's not so bad at the moment, because the wind's more from the south east, but when it's in this direction, straight off the sea . . . Oh dear! Of course, if we had proper, modern windows fitted, then it would . . . but Leo won't hear of it. He was born here, you know, and that always makes a person sentimental about discomforts, haven't you noticed? And of course he's not here half the time — off on assignments, or spending nights in our *pied-à-terre* in Ealing. That's one good thing, you know, that might come out of this accident of his. He's going to be stuck here for weeks by the look of things, until the plaster's off, anyway, and with winter coming on, he'll really find out for himself . . . Perhaps after this he won't be so keen on preserving all the draughts as family heirlooms. What do you think?"

As a marital problem, this one concerning family heirlooms was so different from any of mine and Edwin's that I was at a loss for any very helpful response. So I made a few sympathetic noises, and then sought to change the subject.

"That wreck," I said, pointing. "What happened? Is it quite recent?"

"Recent? Oh no. Before my time, anyway. Well before. Every now and then there's a fuss about it, letters in the local paper, that sort of thing. They want it salvaged, you see, or somehow cleared away, it's a maritime hazard, but all the authorities say it's some other authority that ought to pay for it, and so it looks like staying there for ever. Actually, it's becoming a tourist attraction of sorts, an enterprising chap in the village runs boat trips out to it in the season. The visitors love it, they tear off bits of rotten wood to take home and put on their sideboards. 'From a real wreck.' You know. *Trippers*. They love that sort of thing."

"It hardly looks far enough out for a boat trip," I remarked. "From here, it looks as if you could just about paddle out to it."

Jessica laughed (the first time, incidentally, I had heard her laugh). "Oh *no*! It's deceptive, you know, the distance. It's the best part of half a mile, I believe, at high tide. Not that I've ever been out there, but my woman knows all about it — of course it's her cousin that runs the trips. It's a bit of lark, she says . . ."

"I hope she's getting better," I interposed, feeling that I should have asked after the lady earlier, but somehow there hadn't been an opportunity. "I hope it isn't anything serious?"

"Serious? Oh *no*. Just her back. She's got to take things easy, the doctor says, which is all very well, but what about *me*? *I* can't take things easy! One thing on top of another, and Leo coming home any day now . . . *My* back will be playing up if I'm not careful, and *then* how will we manage . . . ?"

Thus it came about that by the end of the afternoon I had acquired myself a substantial role in the Coburn ménage. I undertook, for a start, to produce an evening meal for the three of us — no, four, Jessica hastily corrected me, because Rhoda

138

Fairbrother would be dropping in again about the Pageant. That's what she'd come about this morning, actually, but had been side-tracked by finding Edwin here, and him so interested in medieval history. The pageant wasn't till June, actually, but Rhoda was like that, and meantime could I — could I possibly? — see to the geese? She, Jessica, was feeling the beginnings of a tickle in her throat, and it would be just too awful if she was laid up with one of her chests just when Leo was arriving . . .

Geese. Well, there has to be a first time. Under my hostess' instructions, I mixed up a porridgy concoction of coarse meal and kitchen scraps, and carried it out through the old stable-yard beyond the disused wash-house.

The wind hit me as I opened the door and I could scarcely close it behind me against the force of the rising gale.

"They'll be in the top meadow," Jessica had said, with an explanatory wave of the hand in the required direction, and so thither I made my way, almost losing my breath as I battled against the wind.

The meadow was large and neglected, overgrown with tall thistles, but as to locating the geese, there was no problem: they were already gathered in a tight phalanx athwart the gate, and at the sight of me and my bucket they set up that hysterical whispering which is the goose equivalent of a rousing cheer.

I had been instructed not to feed them until they were inside the untidy structure of chicken-wire and corrugated iron which protected them at night from foxes, rats, and the sheer force of rain and wind; and so with some trepidation I pushed and waded my way through the hissing, frantic concourse, surprised — townswoman as I am — at the gentleness of the soft little pecks which came my way as the snake-like heads tried to thrust themselves into my bucket.

I won through in the end; when it came to the crunch, I was bigger than they were — and within a very few minutes my charges were safely inside, guzzling, gulping and gasping in rapture, while with chilled fingers I was fastening the compli-

139

cated contraption of wire, staples and metal hooks which secured the door.

The journey back across the field was a whole lot easier; no geese going spare around my ankles, and the wind behind me. Jauntily, I swung my empty bucket, the wind catching it like a sail on every up-swing; and it wasn't until I reached the gate that I realised I was being watched.

"Where have you been? What the hell are you doing?"

Edwin's voice was sharp with outrage — or was it fear? — and I was startled, naturally. But the hugeness of the wind, the sky, the vast spaces, was still with me, and I simply laughed. Yes, I laughed; he looked so furtive, so guilty, and — yes — so trivial, somehow. What did I care? He was up to something, obviously, but it couldn't be anything very dire, because Leonard wasn't even in England yet . . . And just look at that sky, the huge, galloping clouds . . . !

And so I laughed. His face, already pinched with cold (had he been lurking here for some time?) darkened.

"I don't see what's so funny. Where have you been? What have you got in there?"

I swung the empty bucket almost into his face, and laughed again.

"Nothing! Look for yourself! I've been feeding the geese, if you want to know. Jessica asked me to. I don't know why she didn't ask you, if it comes to that. It's a man's job, this sort of thing."

Not true, of course. It's goose-*girls* that crop up in the fairy stories, not goose-boys. And what about the goose that laid the golden egg? Wasn't it the old woman who killed it, which of course is the final stage of looking after a goose. However, the remark sufficed to annoy Edwin. Why I wanted to do this I cannot say; I think it was something to do with the wind whistling into my buzzing, aching ears.

We made our way back to the house in silence, each of us, I suppose, filled to overflowing with thoughts that must be kept hidden from the other.

CHAPTER XXII

Risotto, I decided, was the best solution. One thing Jessica *had* got plenty of was long grain, unpolished rice, though of most other foodstuffs she was running lamentably short. It was impossible to get to the shops, she'd explained, without a car, and since she couldn't drive because of her tranquilisers, and Edwin couldn't because of his car being at this garage, there was nothing, literally nothing, to eat. She had spread her hands despairingly: what should she do? So I had taken up the challenge — well, I could hardly do less, and so now here I was, rooting round her kitchen and into the deepest recesses of her refrigerator. No deep freeze, I noted —was this also due to Leo's having been born here?

Remains of the corned beef. Half a dozen slightly dried-up olives. A heel of cheddar cheese. Oh, but I mustn't use that on account of her anti-depressants. A large Spanish onion, though, and several smaller ones, already sprouting. Tomatoes, too, set to ripen on a window-ledge, some already yellowish, and just about usable if fried. Dandelion leaves for the picking, while the light lasted. Oh, and eggs. Goose eggs, naturally, but also half a dozen hens' eggs in a carton. Which, I asked, would she like me to use?

"*Oh*." She paused, indecision creasing her white brow. "That's a problem, Clare. You see, the goose eggs want eating, no doubt about that, but there's been all this about salmonella:

goose eggs and duck eggs are supposed to be the worst. They were on about it again last night, in *Panorama*; did you watch it?"

I didn't as it happened, and as she could have worked out for herself if she'd thought about it for a moment, because by nine thirty that evening I was already on the train. But it didn't matter, because Jessica was ready and willing to tell me all about the programme: the symptoms, the special danger for the old, the young, the victims of this or that disability, which included — did it? didn't it? — one or more of Jessica's own complaints? Nervous tension? Headaches? Delayed-shock syndrome? What did I think?

I thought (for my own culinary convenience, largely) that these ailments would be of no significance in relation to salmonella poisoning. Jessica seemed to accept this off-the-cuff verdict contentedly enough, warning me, however, that it took fifteen minutes, not seven, to hard-boil a goose egg, and be sure to do them thoroughly because if you don't they tend to taste of fish.

The eggs — I hadn't quite realised how huge they were — had had half their allocated time when the telephone rang. Through the open door I had been listening to Jessica and Edwin chatting companionably about the symptoms of salmonella poisioning. The voices suddenly ceased, and a moment later Jessica's head came round the kitchen door.

"It's for you, Clare," she said. "She seems to want to speak to you, not me. Mrs Barlow — you know, Richard's mother. You can take it in here, if you like, on the extension, so you can watch the eggs at the same time."

"Clare! Oh, thank goodness I've got you. I've been ringing and ringing you at home, I had no idea . . . What are you *doing* up there, if you don't mind my asking? Has something happened to Leonard? — What *is* going on?"

What indeed? Should I tell her — well, you see, my husband is planning to murder your son as soon as he can think up some way of doing it that actually works. He's made some half-baked attempts already; twice trying to cause a motoring accident — then toying with ideas about poisonous fungi; and right now he's learning all he can about salmonella poisoning. This morning he was into ergot, too, but I guess he's given that up as a non-starter. Oh, and why he's here is because he has similar intentions towards Leonard Coburn. The point is, you see, that the story he's been telling on TV and to the world's press is all lies from beginning to end; he never went on the trip at all, as your Richard well knows, and Leonard does too. They are the only two people in the world who know for certain that he is lying, and so he's hell-bent on silencing them before they can get together and show him up. So you see, Daphne . . .

"So you see, Daphne," I heard myself saying aloud, "we got this rather desperate letter from Jessica; she's been ill, and didn't know how she could cope with Leonard's return single handed, and so we felt — well, we both felt — that . . ."

"Yes, yes!" Daphne's tone, usually so controlled and calm, was tense with impatience and anxiety. "Yes, I gathered she was in some sort of difficulty . . . She rang us, you see; that is, she rang Richard — unfortunately I was out at the time — and so I've only got Sally's account of what happened . . ."

She paused here for a fraught second or two, giving me time to translate the remark. 'I've only got Sally's account,' meant, of course, 'I've only got a most woolly, garbled and wildly over-optimistic version of what's going on.'

"Anyway, Clare, the long and the short of it is that Richard has rushed up there, forbidding Sally to accompany him. Apparently they almost had a row about it, and so I know it must be something serious as normally he gives in to Sally about *everything*. There's only one reason why he would put his foot down about her going with him, and that's if he knew he was going into danger. *That's* why I'm worried. Now do you understand?"

All too well. She was dead right, he *was* going into danger. Aloud I said: "Of course I do. I can see how worrying it is for you. What do you . . . ? That is, is there anything *I* can do? Really, I'm

143

just here to help Jessica through a difficult patch, but if there's anything . . . ?"

"Just to let me know when Richard arrives. Get him to ring me *at once*. I'm not asking him to explain anything, I know his work is sometimes highly confidential, and I respect that, I always have; he knows I always have. But just to let me know that he is all right. That he has at least arrived all right. That's all. I hate to play the possessive mother, I just hate it, it's not me at all, but when it's a question of real danger . . ."

Yes, indeed. In the same way, I was going to hate playing the possessive wife during that drive to the airport. Again, real danger. Fear is the parent of possessiveness. Always has been.

"Of course I'll get him to ring," I assured her. "Though he may be staying in a hotel, you know; he wouldn't necessarily come straight here, even if he *is* planning to meet up with Leonard — which I suppose he must be. Anyway, as soon as I know anything, I'll ring you. OK?"

But as it happened, it was she who rang me. Only an hour or so later, just as we were finishing the last of the risotto, which had really turned out surprisingly successful.

It was Jessica who picked up the receiver, and she handed it to me almost at once. Daphne's voice had a stiff, taut quality which was quite frightening. It sounded as if she was talking with teeth clenched, exercising almost superhuman control.

Sally, too, had disappeared now. *With* Barnaby. No, she had left no note. Nothing.

CHAPTER XXIII

Our room looked larger than ever, and full of shadows, when we came up to bed late that evening. The double bed was a problem; it always is when we are confronted with one away from home after a day of holiday bickering. Still, we have grown used to it over the years, and have tacitly evolved a technique for dealing with it, after a fashion. Politeness. Coolness. Please and Thank you. Do you mind if . . . ?

Rather the same, I suppose, as sharing a cabin with a stranger on a Channel crossing. Restful in a way, compared with actual communication.

But on this occasion, we were barely into the opening moves of this ploy when we were interrupted by an urgent knock on the door, followed by the entrance of Jessica in a lacy coffee-coloured négligé, and with her glossy black hair swinging loose about her shoulders.

"Oh, dear, I'm so sorry," she apologised, "I thought I'd remembered everything and taken all the things I was going to need, but I find I'm down to my last Temazepam! Just one left, I shan't get a wink of sleep with only one, and so I'll have to fall back on my Mogadons . . ."

She had crossed the room as she spoke, and had pulled open one of the small top drawers of the chest of drawers. From where I stood, I could see that it was filled almost to overflowing with an amazing assortment of bottles, jars and phials; tins of throat lozenges, indigestion pills, vitamin supplements, the lot. Con-

145

fidently, she plunged her hand into the recesses of the drawer — she seemed to know, amazingly, exactly where to find the required bottle among all this chaos.

But apparently she was mistaken.

"Oh dear!" She withdrew her hand, looking momentarily bemused. "I could have sworn . . . I wonder, though . . . ?" Again the hand immersed itself in the medley of medicaments. The containers rattled and clinked against one another.

"Though of course," she remarked, as she continued her search. "Mogadons aren't nearly as good as Temazepams, not so strong, I'll have to take extra. That's why my doctor prescribes me the Temazepams now; he said that three Mogadons was too many. They build up in your system, he says, and they can affect your eyes if you keep on with them for years, which would be awful, of course. But just now and again it can't hurt, can it and that's why I've kept them, in case I run out of my proper ones . . . Oh dear, where *can* they be . . . ?"

At last, she gave up, shutting the drawer with an irritable slam.

"Oh well, I suppose I'll have to make do with my tranks. It's not the same . . . not a bit the same . . . and just when I *need* a decent night's sleep! All the things I'm going to have to see to tomorrow . . . I don't know how I shall get through the day if I don't get a decent night's sleep . . ."

There was no way I could help — well, no way I *dared* help, anyway, whatever my suspicions. I didn't look at Edwin, and he didn't look at me. After she had gone, I summoned all my courage to ask him — still not looking him in the eye — whether he had by any chance come across the pills, somewhere about the room?

"Of course not!" he snapped. "Why should you think such a thing? I'd have told her, wouldn't I, not left her scrabbling around like that. It was a bloody nuisance, if you ask me. Do you realise it's after midnight?"

A bloody nuisance indeed. Just when he thought the time had come when he could safely purloin the pills, his hostess had to come barging in like that and start searching for them.

What should I do? Accuse him to his face? The only outcome of this would be yet more furious denials. And of course I had no *proof* that he had taken them. I just knew it, that's all.

Also, to accuse him point-blank would assuredly put him on his guard, and make my self-appointed task of keeping an eye on him even more difficult.

Keeping an eye on him. An unsleeping eye, ideally, but this was impossible. I'd been up all night last night, I couldn't possibly stay awake tonight as well.

Besides, Leonard wasn't here yet. Nothing could happen until he came.

Tonight, I must sleep, and sleep and sleep . . .

I woke barely an hour later with the feeling that I had been roused suddenly by someone talking, right here in the room.

I lay very still. No, it wasn't Edwin; in his tacitly allotted fifty per cent of the bed he was breathing deeply, evenly, and I could tell that he was sleeping soundly, not pretending. Luckily, he is not very good at pretending, I can tell at once.

The voice — if it had indeed been a voice — had ceased; had I dreamed it, then?

And then, without warning, it all started again, right here, only inches from my ear, and for one terrifying moment I thought I had gone mad, was hallucinating — ergot, or something . . .

"Who is the person in your life you love most?" a seductive male voice was crooning into my ear. "Your husband, you say? —Wrong! Your child, then? Your mother? Wrong again! Your lover? Wrong, Wrong, Wrong! The person you must love most is *yourself*! Unless you love yourself, you can love no one . . ."

It was coming along the pipes in the wall, I realised now, right behind the draped bedhead. Somewhere, an all-night radio programme was on. The assortment of soporifics to which Jessica had treated herself had evidently not been enough, and she was whiling away the sleepless hours with the radio.

It was a relief, of course, to realise that I hadn't gone mad, but of course that didn't stop it being annoying. It was a woman this time:

"It may look easy, but once you are up here, with only a thin wire between you and a hundred-foot drop . . ."

How could it possibly look easy, whatever it was? It crossed my mind to go and remonstrate with our hostess, to point out to her that a programme designed to be soothing to insomniacs wasn't soothing at all to people whose habit it was to sleep at night.

But I thought better of it. Her nerves were in a bad way already, by all accounts, and if the sleeping pills weren't working for her, then it would be cruel to deprive her of such solace as this purpose-built programme could provide.

"And do remember that it may not be cancer at all. In fact, it almost certainly isn't. Of the two thousand or so worried women who turn up at our clinic each week, less than . . ."

Of course, I reflected, a great wave of irritation meeting head-on with a counter-wave of drowsiness inside my skull, of course, she doesn't realise: she has no idea that the sound is carrying through the wall like this, she's not really being inconsiderate.

So what was she really being? Something about plastic bottles now, that you should save them for recycling, or perhaps that you shouldn't. I was in a kind of a dream by now, all those plastic bottles leaning precariously against each other on that high shelf, someone should do something, they were obviously about to fall. "Casting off!" cried the first one decisively as it clattered onto the floor, click click, clatter clatter, click . . . "For casting *off* you should use a smaller size needle than the one you used in the pattern; for casting *on*, a larger one. This way, you get a neater, firmer edge . . ."

Neater. Firmer. She can say that again. Trying to get things neater and firmer is the story of my life. Perhaps of everyone's. Next thing I knew, someone was reciting 'Under the faraway, faraway tree', which soon turned into a talk about Pissarro, or was it pistachios; whichever it was I couldn't see what that nice little bit of a Chopin prelude could have to do with it, except that it had been asked for by a Mr William Willis of Dorking . . .

It must have been nearly three o'clock when the chattering voices at last fell silent. Perhaps Jessica had got fed up with them herself, and had switched them off; or perhaps they had finally come to the end of everything that could possibly be said to soften all those brains rigid with wakefulness and to lead the weary band of the nation's insomniacs into unconsciousness?

Whatever the reason, it was a huge relief, and with the onset of blessed silence I felt sleep rushing over me in unstoppable waves.

An hour? — two hours later? I don't know. At first, I thought it was the radio voices starting up again, and I cursed as I felt myself being dragged kicking and screaming back into consciousness. This was too much! It was beyond bearing! This time, I really *would* . . .

And then, suddenly, I was fully awake, every nerve alert, every muscle at the ready. Something was happening. Edwin was no longer here, and the sound that had roused me — yes, here it was again:

"Leo! Leo! Oh no! *No!*"

Jessica's voice, shrill with terror "No! No!"

I was out of bed and out on the dark landing barefoot and in my nightdress, groping wildly in the direction from which I had heard the cry coming.

But which door? This door? That door? Oh, for a light! My hand, crab-like, clawed its way this way and that, up and down the uncharted stretches of unfamiliar wall.

"It's all right, Jessica, I'm coming!" I called into the darkness, though what I meant to convey by 'all right' I cannot imagine. It's all right, it's only Edwin murdering your husband under your very eyes. It's all right, your husband has only gone mad as

149

a result of concussion and is murdering *you*. It's all right. It's all right, Clare is coming. Or would be if she could only find the bloody light switch . . .

My bare toe stubbed against some recalcitrant wooden obstacle — an old oak dower chest I discovered in the morning — and while the pain paused for that eerie second that it takes to travel from the toe to the pain-centres in the brain, a thin streak of light flared across the darkness through the crack in a nearby door, and I plunged headlong towards it, and into the room beyond.

Jessica was sitting up in bed, blinking, breathing in short, panicky gasps and looking incongruously glamorous in the rosy light from her bedside lamp, her swathes of luxuriant black hair falling across her bare shoulders.

No scene of bloodshed. Neither her husband nor mine was standing, knife in hand, poised to strike.

"I'm so sorry, Clare," she said, her voice now quite normal and composed. "Did I wake you? It happens sometimes. I didn't mean to, but I had this awful dream and I couldn't stop myself screaming. It's these pills, you know" — she reached across her bedside table towards a plastic container and shook it irritably. "If only I had my proper pills, this wouldn't happen. The doctor did say not to take these any more, but I hadn't anything else as I'd forgotten to phone up about a repeat prescription. These are the ones that tend to give me nightmares — Oh, Clare, it was so awful! I'm still shaking — look!" She held out her white, slender hand towards me, and I clasped it, trying to convey reassurance, for it was indeed trembling.

"It's all right," I said, yet again, and still somewhat at random. "It's all right now." And then:

"What was it? You were calling out for Leo — he's not here, is he? He hasn't come back?"

"No, no. Of course he hasn't. He can't possibly be here until tomorrow or the next day. It was only a dream . . . but, oh, Clare, it was such an awful dream! I dreamed he was here, standing beside the bed, smiling down at me. He was wearing his anorak, just like when he went away, and I knew I should be so pleased to see him, but I couldn't be, because I knew that there was something wrong. 'Leo,' I said, 'What's happened? What's the matter?' He opened his mouth to answer, but what came out of it wasn't words, but an awful whining, which went on and on. And his smile became full of teeth, great yellow teeth, turning into fangs while I watched, and I knew then that he had turned into a werewolf. Someone had given him ergot, and I hadn't got the antidote. I needed a prescription . . . Oh dear, isn't it mad the way things get mixed up in dreams?" She laughed a little, apologetically. "Anyway, the next thing, I found myself screaming. I'm so sorry, Clare, it must have scared you dreadfully . . ."

She was calmer now, assuring me that she would be all right. All the same, I stayed with her until she fell asleep, as if she was a child. Then, very quietly, I tiptoed back to bed. Edwin was still not there, and as well as I could for weariness, I tried to worry about it. But what could I do? Where could I look for him? What might he be up to?

It dawned on me then that he must have been wakened, just before I was, by Jessica's first cry of 'Leo! Leo!' He must have imagined that the man really had arrived back in the middle of the night. Right now, he would be lurking somewhere, still in his pyjamas, freezing cold, preparing himself for an encounter that wasn't going to happen.

It would be funny if it hadn't been so frightening, but neither fear nor laughter was any match for the total exhaustion that now overcame me, and I sank into a sleep so deep that it was just like being dead. Well, like my idea of being dead, anyway: the same sense of total escape: of having gone beyond the range of absolutely everything, into a place where no one can get at you, nothing be demanded of you, ever again.

When at length I woke, it was past nine o'clock. The wind had

151

dropped, the sun was streaming in dazzlingly through the lattice window, and from downstairs came the reassuring sounds of a household already astir.

CHAPTER XXIV

I wasn't finding the task of shopping without a car nearly as daunting as Jessica had made it sound. The village shop sold just about everything, including the things you can't get for love or money in London, like narrow black elastic and reels of cotton. Jessica had left most of the decisions to me: something for today's lunch, she'd said, and then something for the evening meal as well. "Something really nice," she urged, "just in case Leo might be back, though I don't suppose he will be. It might easily not be till tomorrow or Friday." Someone from the hospital was supposed to be calling her, but it hadn't happened yet, so all she could do was stay by the telephone and hope. Well, all *she* could do. Someone else might have found something more positive to do with the time, such as ringing the hospital herself despite the problems of language and foreign exchanges: but Jessica was Jessica, and changing her nature was no part of my duties as a cooperative guest. Besides, what about that tickle in her throat? She still had it, no worse, but likewise no better, as is the way with tickles in the throat after barely half a day.

Bread. Milk. Sausages. Such little pies as they had in stock, and as many tins of variegated goodies as I felt I could reasonably be expected to lug home in the two shopping bags, one on each arm.

Thus weighed down, I paused outside the shop to consider my route. Straight back along the road would be quickest, but I felt a great yearning to walk alongside the sea, the final gusts of last

153

night's gale whipping my hair; and so, despite my load, I turned left, and set off in the direction of the shore.

The tide was far out, and I saw them first when they were still almost half a mile away, three solitary little figures standing out black and tiny in the expanse of empty sand. At this distance I could not see what they were doing, their movements were minuscule, aimless, like those of ants; and it was only after several more minutes of walking along the restless white margin of the ebbing tide that I was able to recognise them with any certainty. Sally's blonde sweep of hair was tossed by the wind into damp wisps around her bright face; Barnaby was dragging a spade this way and that across the wet sand, bored, making idle patterns while he waited for the grown-ups to *do* something.

And Edwin? He stood a little aside contemplating them both, and I could tell, even at this distance, from the very set of his shoulders, that he was feeling pleased with himself; as if he had scored off something or somebody.

I increased my pace. The shopping bags banged viciously against my thighs as I half-ran towards them.

"Sally!" I cried, as soon as I judged I was within hearing, "what are you *doing*? Daphne's terribly upset; you ought to . . ."

I'd judged the distance wrongly.

"*What*?" she answered, and before I was able to repeat my reprimand, Barnaby had broken away and was racing towards me, the spade swinging at all angles as he ran.

It wasn't as flattering as it looked. He was merely bored, and I was the nearest thing to a happening that had come his way for many a long minute.

The flailing spade landed on my ankle, edgewise.

"Ouch!" I said. "Didn't mean to," he perfunctorily apologised; and then, oppressed by the realisation that one grown-up is just as dull as another when they are intent on their own affairs, he turned and sauntered back to his former companions.

Sally reached out and clutched Edwin's hand, as if seeking

moral support in the face of my reproaches, which she must have seen were justified.

"Yes, well, I suppose I *should* have left her a note, but I took for granted she'd *know* where I'd gone. I mean, she knew Richard and I had been having a bit of a thing about it; I told her. He was being so funny about not letting me come with him, you see; I don't know what got into him. I mean, it seemed such a wicked shame, a lovely seaside place like this, and not to take me and Barnaby . . . We never had a proper holiday this year, you know, with all the to-ings and fro-ings and terrorists and stuff, and so this seemed such a chance . . . And so in the end we just *came!*" she finished. "Didn't we, Barnaby? On the *train* . . ."

"*Two* trains," Barnaby corrected her. "An Inter-city and then . . ."

"And then of course we had to get a taxi," Sally resumed the narrative, "and I found I hadn't got enough money. The man wanted another three pounds forty, and so when we got to the hotel Richard had to come down and pay him . . . It was a pity it had to happen that way . . . I'd planned to give him a lovely surprise, bursting into his room and giving him a lovely great kiss. It's difficult, that sort of thing, while you're paying a taxi."

Her voice trailed away, and I gathered that the reunion hadn't been a great success.

"But it's all right *now*," she finished. "He's as pleased as pleased to have me with him, I knew he would be, he always is in the end . . . Barnaby, why don't you run on ahead and see if Daddy's finished showing Jessica all those papers . . . ?"

We were nearing the top of the beach now, and Sally, still swinging Edwin's hand light-heartedly in her own, was kicking with her bare feet at the dry, powdery sand, carefree as a child.

"What a gorgeous morning!" she cried, tossing her bright head. "It's like magic, isn't it, all this sun and wind. Poor Richard! What a shame he's spending the whole lovely morning indoors with all that silly work!"

155

He wasn't, though. By this time, Barnaby, scrambling, slipping and battling his way up the steep sand dune ahead of us, had let out a cry of delight and surprise.

"Daddy!" he shrieked, "Daddy, what you doing? Daddy, get *up*!"

And Daddy (I suppose by now there was no other option) got up. His tall spare figure rose with dignity from the clump of marram grass by which it had been concealed.

Had he been watching us? Or merely resting, enjoying the view? He moved in our direction, awkwardly of course as he negotiated the steep slope of the dune, but when he reached the level surface of the beach, I noticed that his movements were still awkward. His limping was more noticeable than it had been in London, and as he drew near, I could see that his face was pale and strained. He looked almost ill.

However, he said nothing about being in pain — well, he wouldn't, would he? — and his perfect manners were still in place. He greeted both me and Edwin with punctilious correctness, and soon our ill-assorted little party were setting off together towards the house.

"What those big ducks going to do?" enquired Barnaby, clutching his father's hand and pulling back as we reached the meadow gate. "I don't like those big ducks!"

"Geese," corrected his father, tightening his grip on the child's hand and pulling him forward. "Come along, Barnaby, they won't hurt you."

"They *will* hurt me!" Barnaby balked and pulled back harder than ever. "They're cross! They're *saying* that they're cross!"

And it did indeed sound like that. Ever-hopeful, even though it was hours before their normal feeding-time, the whole flock had gathered in force at our approach, and their greedy, reproachful hissing did indeed sound threatening — especially when it was head-high to the listener as it was to Barnaby.

"No . . . ! No . . . !" he wailed, but his father — shamed, I

could see, by this public display of pusillanimity by his only son—
dragged him forward.

A light tap on the child's leg from one of the roving beaks was the last straw. Barnaby burst into howls of fear and indignation, while his father, frowning, seemed to decide that the upholding of the family honour was not being best served by a continuance of the battle. He gave up, and allowed the boy to retreat a pace or two.

He was not pleased, however, and reproved the child quite sharply:

"Stop crying, Barnaby! Don't be so silly! Stop it at once! Big boys don't cry!"

The large tear-filled blue eyes were raised to the father's dark and stern ones:

"Big boys *do* cry! *I'm* a big boy, and *I'm* crying!" he countered, with unassailable logic; and at this fraught moment of father-son relations, Edwin saw fit to intervene.

"I'll tell you what, Barnaby," he said, holding out an encouraging hand, "All we have to do is to march slowly through them, saying, very loudly, 'Geese, geese, let us through! Geese, geese, let us through!' We have to say it both together while we march—Like this!"

And lo and behold, chanting this mantra at the top of their voices, the two of them tramped through the concourse quite unscathed.

"Again! Again!" shrieked Barnaby, tears dried, his face alight. "Let's march through them *again*, Edwin!"

And hand in hand, their faces aglow with triumph, the two of them paced back and forth through the flock twice more.

Barnaby was in ecstasy: Edwin hardly less so, visibly preening himself on the fact that he had displayed child-handling skills far superior to those of the boy's own father.

And Richard? For a fraction of a second, I saw such hatred in his eyes as I have never before witnessed. But the look was gone almost before I had registered it, replaced by the usual cool, controlled and dignified demeanour.

And within seconds, Sally had put things even further to rights — whether through loving insight into her husband's feelings, or simply through a spontaneous overflow of exuberance from her own sunny nature, I could not guess. Whichever it was, she did exactly the right thing: nestling up against Richard as they walked, and changing the subject entirely with a bit of special pleading.

"Darling," she said, "you know what I'd simply *love* to do while we're here? Oh, do say we can . . . You can't be working *all* the time, now can you?"

The light, the softness that came into the strained, stern face as he looked down at her was lovely to behold.

"What is it, pet?" he asked. "Something within reason, I trust?" And you could tell from the smile in his voice that it would need to be something far outside reason indeed before he would find it in his heart to refuse.

"That wreck," Sally was explaining eagerly. "That wreck we saw from our hotel window — remember? And you were wondering how it had got there — why they hadn't done something about it — ?"

"Well? And you've found out, have you, love?"

"Sort of, yes, at least what I *have* found out is that they run boat trips round it! That woman at our table at breakfast — she says the official trips are over for the season, but she thinks you can still hire a boat and row yourself out. Oh, Richard, do let's! It would be such fun!"

"Well . . ." Richard was still smiling, longing to please her, but nevertheless a little cautious. "I'll have to find out about it. The currents may be very treacherous, you see, round a massive obstacle like that. For anyone who doesn't know the coast . . . isn't familiar with the tides . . ."

"Oh, darling, don't be such an old *stick*! *Of course* it'll be all right! I mean, they wouldn't hire out the boats, would they, unless . . ."

"And another thing, Sally. A lot depends on when Leonard is

due to arrive. That's the main reason for our being here, to help Jessica with things like driving to the airport. He'll still be a bit of an invalid, you know, and I'm rather anxious to . . ."

"Oh, darling, *of course.*" Sally concurred. "Of course that must come first. But, I mean, he won't be arriving *all the time*, will he? I mean, if he arrives today, then he won't be arriving tomorrow, will he? And if he's arriving tomorrow, then this afternoon we could . . ."

She chattered on, happy and full of plans. Listening to her, I felt a surge of relief. So it would be *Richard* driving Jessica to the airport, not Edwin at all. My anxieties on this score had been quite superfluous.

A few minutes later, we had reached the house, and Jessica, despite her throat (or had it perhaps stopped tickling now, cured by excitement?) was hurrying out to meet us.

"I've heard!" she cried. "They've telephoned, and his plane should be getting in at 2.55! We'll just have time for a very quick lunch . . . Oh, isn't it exciting? . . . Oh dear, there's so much I haven't done! It's all so difficult, and Phoebe hasn't arrived today *at all*! She's so unreliable, that girl, it's really hardly worth . . . And I meant to have *such* a nice meal ready for him, his first evening . . . !"

There followed a distracting few minutes of suggestions and counter-suggestions; arrangements about places, starting times, and whether the Barlows should or should not stay and have lunch here, despite there being only three small pork pies and some celery? And there was the further question; whether Barnaby should be allowed to share in the jaunt to the airport? He would be in the way, Richard maintained; on the other hand, said Sally, he would love to see the planes landing and taking off; and anyway, what else was to be done with him?

This was my cue, I couldn't help feeling, to offer to baby sit for the afternoon, though with no great enthusiasm. I had already undertaken to contrive some sort of celebration meal for the returning hero, which would almost certainly involve a further

159

visit to the village shop; to do all this with Barnaby at my heels was a daunting prospect; and so I was greatly relieved when Sally changed tack, apparently quite willingly, and suggested that she herself should stay behind and look after her small son. It would leave more room for Leo, wouldn't it, in case he needed to put his injured leg up on the back seat.

It was while all this was being settled that I noticed, for the first time, that Edwin was no longer with us. Had he gone on indoors? Or lagged behind in the meadow? Or . . . ?

CHAPTER XXV

I remembered exactly where I had found our car yesterday, and now, as I hurried along the coast road in the hazy afternoon warmth, I was no longer puzzled as to why Edwin had chosen to park it there, and bother to lie about its whereabouts as well. He had been scheming all the time to drive to the airport alone when the time came, to meet Leonard Coburn by himself, before anyone else had a chance to do so. Had he brought the car right up to the house, and parked it in the stable-yard, or in the road just outside, he would have had no chance whatever of driving off unnoticed. Inevitably, Jessica would have joined him; would have assumed, naturally, that giving her a lift was the whole purpose of the expedition.

Exactly as I had expected. Deep tyre-marks were still visible on the sandy verge, but the car was gone.

For a few moments I stood baffled, bathed in the weak sunshine, and trying to work out, from the data available, what Edwin might be planning to do?

I let the scenario wash over me. Edwin, all smiles and handshakes, greeting his erstwhile colleague. What about a drink, old boy, before we set off? A beer? A double whisky? Or do you feel more like a coffee? No, no, you just sit here, I'll get it . . .

And then, on the way back from the bar, or from the tea and coffee counter, there would be a small detour past some inconspicuous table where he could set the drinks down and shake into one of them the ready-crushed Mogadons. Who, among the bustling, self-absorbed passengers was going to notice or care what a total stranger was doing with his tray of drinks?

Not a fatal dose, of course. This is not possible with Mogadon anyway, as is surely well known: well known to Edwin, anyway, so assiduous had been his medical researches of late. Not a fatal dose, then, but enough to make his victim bemused and drowsy, possibly comatose, so that his state on arriving home would endorse one hundred percent Edwin's carefully planted predictions about the dire effects of concussion. Leonard, of course, would begin to recover at some stage during the evening or night: but who would thereafter give total credence to the assertions of a man who could fall so easily and so unpredictably into a state of semi-consciousness?

Something like that. And what in the world could I do to prevent it? Edwin had had already a good half-hour's start: there was no way I could catch up with him now even if, miraculously, a hired car should be available at a moment's notice in this out-of-the-way spot. I could, of course, go back to the house and beg to be taken along with the others in Richard's car. No one would object, I felt sure.

Here I was brought up short, my colourful scenario falling about my ears. Edwin might indeed reach the airport ahead of the others, but what would he gain by that? It would merely involve him in waiting an extra length of time in the Arrival bay until Leonard's plane came in, by which time the others would be waiting too, probably standing alongside, and his early, furtive start would have achieved nothing.

Surely, surely, Edwin would have thought of this?

He had. When I reached the house some minutes later, I found an angry, chattering little crowd gathered round Richard's car, which was parked in the cobbled yard. Our own party were all there, augmented by the freckle-faced Phoebe (who had evidently devised some way of missing school after all), and also by our local historian, Rhoda Fairbrother, of werewolf fame.

Even My Woman was amongst the throng, apparently risen from her bed of sickness for the occasion.

"It's those lager louts from Milham Bridge!" Rhoda was angrily asserting. "None of *our* lads would do a thing like that! It's the parents, you know; Milham Bridge is turning into one of those commuting villages, the parents working in London, out of the house till nine o'clock at night, the mothers too. No time for their kids at all. It's no wonder . . ."

In the midst of this sociological diagnosis, Richard, crimson-faced, was struggling to change the wheel, receiving minimal help from the surrounding company: not from lack of goodwill, or even of efficiency; rather from a multiplicity of good intentions, each tending to cancel out the other.

"No, Jessica, more to the right. Sally, darling, move *away!* You're preventing . . . Now, when I say 'Three' . . . All together . . ."

The fixing of the spare wheel seemed to be presenting some unforeseen problem. The original one, ferociously slashed, lay in the dust. I watched, anxiously. Time was passing.

"What about *your* car, Jessica?" I tentatively suggested. "Just this once . . . ?"

She shook her head, miserably. "It's having its overhaul," she explained. "Since I can't drive at the moment, it seemed a good time to . . .

At last, the wheel was fixed. I looked at my watch. They were bound to be late, but maybe the plane wouldn't be on time.

In another few minutes, they were on their way, the rest of us standing at the gate, waving, and watching them gather speed along the coast road.

Why hadn't I done anything? Why hadn't I warned them of what Edwin was planning to do? Wasn't this taking wifely loyalty altogether too far? How could I allow Leo's mental stability to be so unjustly called into question? Well, I wouldn't allow it, I told myself. Not if it actually happened.

But would it? The scenario I'd conjured up did seem to be the

163

only one which made sense of the purloining of the pills and of Edwin's behaviour this afternoon. I felt little doubt that I had assessed his intentions more or less correctly — but would he, in fact, carry out his plan when it came to the point? Or would he 'get cold feet' as Richard had so scornfully predicted. Would he muddle it somehow? So far, watching from the side-lines, I had several times witnessed what appeared to be murder plans going off at half-cock. Two attempts to involve Richard in a motoring accident; and then the appropriating of Jason's boletus to find out if it was poisonous. What, exactly, had he meant to do if it had turned out that this *was* the case? A lunch party of sorts? At home, or at the Barlows'? With fried mushrooms somehow inserted into the menu?

None of these schemes had so far come to anything, nor (it seemed to me) had had any realistic chance of doing so. Was one not drawn to conclude that at some deep and perhaps unconscious level they hadn't been meant to come to anything? Were they perhaps just as much fantasy as the original fantasy of his non-existent adventures? Just as he had lost his nerve when it came to actually embarking on the dangerous trip with his colleagues, did he also lose his nerve every time one of his murder plans looked as if it might actually work?

Was this why I had been finding it so impossible either to challenge him myself or to warn his potential victims? It was because he hadn't visibly done anything. He hadn't even threatened anyone. How can you accuse a man of violent crime when no violent crime has been committed? The only crime I could accuse him of was the crime of Dangerous Thoughts, and this, surely, only counts as a criminal offence under the most tyrannous of dictatorships? Once again, I came to the conclusion that all I could do was to wait on events. *If* Leo seemed to be in any sort of a daze as he climbed from Edwin's car, then of course I'd . . .

"Come on, Clare, we've made some tea. They won't get back any the sooner for you standing mooning at the gate, you know!"

Rhoda's bracing voice recalled me from my uneasy musings, and I joined the others round the kitchen table for what turned out to be a really quite relaxing half-hour of idle chatter. Sally talked about the hotel she and Richard were staying in, with its darling little mobiles just inside the front door. Rhoda talked about the teenage drug scene in villages other than this one: and My Woman talked about her back, and how it wasn't too bad on the level, it was going up and down stairs that gave her gyp: while Phoebe didn't talk at all, but got on with the homework she had somehow failed to find a way of missing.

By now, Barnaby's afternoon rest was coming to an end. The bumps, scrapes, rattles and thuds that had marked its continuance abruptly ceased, and he was now on his way downstairs, singing loudly to himself, and raring to go.

Go where? Well, there was quite a bit of sunshine still left, Sally calculated, so she could take him on the beach for an hour or so. The plane was bound to be late, Richard wouldn't be back for ages, and if by any chance he *did* turn up, then one of us could tell him he'd find her on the beach. With which carefree assessment of the situation she set off, with Barnaby in her wake, clonking his spade across the cobbles of the stable-yard as they went.

Too many cooks were by now gathering to spoil the coq au vin which I'd planned for Leo's home-coming. It was Rhoda who had come to our rescue in the first place, fetching chicken pieces out of her deepfreeze, and this of course entitled her to interfere in a big way with my plans for cooking it. *No*, she said, leaning across me, marinading them in the wine and bay leaves before cooking wasn't at all necessary, she never bothered with it herself. And why only bay leaves? Surely mixed herbs would give more flavour? And the onions should go in *whole*, not chopped like that.

And My Woman wasn't much better. Naturally enough, she felt herself to have long-established rights over this kitchen, and to every utensil I touched, every pan I reached for, she would say: "No, no, Mrs Coburn always uses *this* one." The problem was compounded by the fact that I didn't know if she was officially back at work, being paid by the hour for hanging about like this, or whether she was just filling in time in order not to miss the excitement of Mr Coburn's return, with his leg in plaster, or so she'd heard and whatever else. In any case, it wasn't for *me* to say Well, thank you very much, I think that'll be all.

The dispute about the chopping and the non-chopping of the onions had just about reached deadlock. It was no longer any use for me just to give in about it, because by now the two of them, Rhoda and My Woman, had established entrenched positions one on each side of the great divide. And so it came about that I felt nothing but relief when the telephone interrupted our preparations. I abandoned the battle-front with alacrity. Let the best chef win.

A lightening strike of air-controllers at some distant airport. Leonard's departure indefinitely delayed. Nothing for it but to come straight back, and wait for further information.

Richard's cool, clipped voice down the telephone gave nothing away of what he was feeling; but obviously he must be considerably put-out and concerned. It came to me that Sally really must be here to greet him when he arrived back, disappointed and on edge. For him to be greeted merely by the casual message that he'd find her on the beach didn't seem a good idea at all.

Come to that, I'd expected them back before now myself. The sun was gone, a chill wind had come up, and clouds were gathering.

At first, as I came down the dunes on to the beach, the place seemed totally deserted. As far as I could see in each direction there was nothing but a grey-brown waste of sand, gleaming wetly where the grey waves rolled in, whipped by the wind into spiralling twists of foam.

166

And then I saw them. Far out on the heaving water, close alongside the wreck. The little boat was tossing and heaving perilously, and the two figures within it leaned and swayed this way and that as they desperately plied their oars. Well, it looked desperate from here, but maybe they knew what they were doing? Edwin has never been what you could call a rowing man, but on our occasional boating trips on holiday, he had always seemed to acquit himself well enough. Until, that is, Jason became old enough to take one of the oars, after which these trips became a nightmare of shouts and scoldings, with Jason, ceaselessly reprimanded, becoming sullen and nervous and beginning actually to do the wrong thing, his steering all to pieces, the boat spinning out of control.

But of course it wouldn't be like that with Sally. Whatever *she* might be doing wrong out in that pitching little craft would be smilingly forgiven — unless, of course, they actually *were* in danger? In which case . . .

My heart lurched. Barnaby . . . ? Was *he* there, with them? Had they ventured to take him, too, on this scatterbrained jaunt? I remembered what Richard had said this morning about the possible danger from currents, the powerful underflow around the wreck. Had it right now got them in its grip, dragging them relentlessly — whither? To their deaths, sucked unstoppably beneath those huge, rotting timbers?

Over the rolling expanse of intervening water I could just distinguish their voices, which at first had so blended with the cries of the gulls and the swirl of the hurrying surf that they had not registered on my hearing. Even now I could not hear what they were saying, nor even the tone of voice, whether of panic or enjoyment. Except, suddenly, Barnaby's voice, shrill and unmistakeable across the racing water:

"Again, Edwin!" I fancied I heard him shriek. "Again! Again!"

So it was all just fun after all? An amusing little adventure, no cause for panic? Or was it just Barnaby who was unaware of any cause for panic? For his sake, were they repressing signs of terrible fear?

The repressing of feelings was not characteristic of Sally; and Edwin, though he did try when it was to his advantage, was no good at it. So perhaps they *were* all right? And now, at last, I began to breathe more freely. The distance between me and the little tossing craft was visibly diminishing. Slowly, and perhaps with some difficulty, they were making it to shore.

"Oh, Clare, it was such *fun!*" cried Sally, struggling up the beach, hair, sweater, jeans all soaked with spray. "It was so *exciting!* We thought we were absolutely going to *capsize*, didn't we, Edwin, when that great wave threw us right smack into the wreck? I thought it was going to *swallow* us, it looks so *huge* when you're close to, you've no idea! I thought we'd never get away from it; we rowed and rowed, and every time a great wave would come and heave us back — "

"Like on the swings!" broke in Barnaby. "Right up, high, high, and then down again! Edwin turned us sideways, so that the big waves could *throw* us against the wreck, didn't you, Edwin? Four, five, six, lots of times!"

How much of all this Richard had heard I will never know. He came behind us noiselessly — or was it that the wailing of the wind and the surge of the incoming tide blotted out the sound of his footsteps in the sand?

His voice, slashing into our midst like a hand grenade, was the first we knew of his approach.

Never had I seen him so uninhibitedly angry. His fury extended even towards Sally. What did she think she was *doing*, risking her life — and Barnaby's too — on this lunatic escapade? Hadn't he *told* her that . . .?

"Oh, darling, I know you said you were going to find out about it, currents and tides and things, but you weren't there, you see. And Edwin *was*, he happened to come down on to the beach just after we got there. And there were these boats, all drawn up ready; there wasn't even anyone taking money and all we had to do was just take one. And so we did. We dragged it down to the sea, and we got into it — Oh, darling, it was such *fun*! And we were perfectly safe, truly we were, Edwin is marvellous at managing a boat, really he is . . ."

"I see. He's marvellous. And if, in the interests of being as marvellous as all that, he'd drowned you both . . ."

"Oh, Richard, darling, you're being a silly old thing, you really are! *Of course* we weren't going to be drowned! *Of course* it was safe; Edwin knew it was, or we wouldn't have gone, would we, Edwin? And anyway, here we are, safe and sound, which just proves . . ."

"Do you realise, Sally, that if the tide hadn't happened to be still coming in, you'd never have got back? The current out there . . ."

"Oh, *darling*," she interrupted again, clutching his arm, clinging to it lovingly, but, for once, receiving no answering pressure: "it didn't *happen* to be coming in, Edwin knew it was coming in, didn't you Edwin? I told you, he's marvellous about . . ."

"Yes. I heard you. You've already explained how marvellous he is."

And here Barnaby, who had been following intently the to-and-fro of the altercation, must have caught that look of utter hatred in his father's eyes which I had glimpsed this morning; for he burst into sudden and uncontrollable sobbing.

"Daddy's cross!" he sobbed; and his mother bent down hastily to console him.

"Daddy's not *really* cross, sweetie," she began, "he's only . . ." but the child pushed her roughly away.

"He *is* really cross," he sobbed. "He's *too* cross! He's crosser than a Daddy ought to be!"

He was, too: and perhaps Richard himself realised it. Anyway, he controlled himself, and swung his little son up in his strong arms, and kissed him, albeit with an upper lip all too used to being stiff. But it was enough. Barnaby, reassured, brought his frightened sobbing quickly to an end.

169

"Daddy!" he squealed, "Daddy, be a horse!" and Richard, hoisting the child on to his shoulders, complied, as well as he could with his painful leg.

Barnaby, on his high perch, bounced with joy.

"*Gallop*, Daddy," he cried, "Gallop really fast, like Edwin does!"

CHAPTER XXVI

It was a chastened and rather silent party which wound its way up and over the sandhills towards Coburn's Farm. Richard, having gently and decisively set his child down on the ground, was now striding rapidly ahead, regardless of whatever pain his leg might be causing. For a few paces, Sally tried to keep up with him, but so total was his lack of response to her presence that she soon fell back and rejoined the rest of us.

"I'm sorry about all that fuss," she apologised. "He can be *such* an old worry-guts at times. But never mind, I'll soon bring him round. He never stays cross with me for long. Never!"

"I'm sure he doesn't," I said warmly, and she nodded, smiling, radiating the utter confidence of one who is utterly loved. She glowed with it, basked in it, despite the chilly wind whipping around her soaked clothes; and once again I felt a stab of sharp, uncontrollable envy shooting through me. Though I was glad for her sake. At least, I think I was. In view of what came later, I hope I was. I would hate to think that any envious thought of mine had spoiled that moment for her, her bare, brown feet happily scuffling through the soft, still-warm sand.

By the time we reached the house, the new moon had come into view, white and thread-like above the tussocky crest of the sandhills behind us; and at the door, by some tacit agreement, we turned and paused, just looking. The sky had cleared, it was not yet dark, and the pure silvery green was pricked as yet by only the brightest stars. Sirius, low down on the south-eastern horizon, and Jupiter right above the roof of the old stable.

I have wondered, since, what Edwin was actually thinking as the three cf us stood taking in the incomparable beauty of it all. Or what was *I* thinking, come to that. Such parallel anxieties were surely preying on us both, parallel lines that never meet. And Sally? She, I hope and think, was simply enjoying a nice bit of her holiday. Leaning with effortless grace against the door jamb, her perfect profile tilted skywards, her bright hair floating, she was perhaps enjoying the beauty of the scene less consciously than I was, being herself a part of it. That feeling of participation in all things lovely is vouchsafed for a little while to the very young, the totally loved, and the effortlessly beautiful.

I hope so, anyway, I hope it was like that for her. I shall always hope so.

The coq au vin was a fair success, despite the vicissitudes attendant on its creation. Rhoda had finished the preparations in *her* way, and I could hardly complain, having abandoned my post as head cook so precipitately; though I *certainly* wouldn't have added all those cloves. One or two, yes, but not so that you got one in almost every mouthful.

Not that it mattered much. Leo not having arrived after all, it was no longer a celebration meal, and didn't have to be perfect. Nor did the conversation have to be particularly jolly; which was just as well, because the atmosphere, dulled by a sense of anticlimax, was subdued, heavy with unspoken thoughts. Laboriously, we made conversation — well, we women did. The men, as so often happens, seemed to feel no social obligation to keep things going, they just concentrated on their food, keeping their eyes down.

Things got just a little easier as the coq au vin came to an end and the trifle was brought in. No one had bothered to decorate it since Leo wasn't here, but it was still very nice — and the talk became almost lively over the question of whether it was easier to keep a dog in London or in the country. The obvious answer, 'in the country', was getting a severe going-over from Rhoda. What with the sheep, and the bird sanctuary, and the rabbit snares, and the shooting, and the lorries charging along narrow lanes, a dog not kept on a lead will either be dead or have landed its owner in court within a . . .

And at this point, the phone went. For me again: Daphne; and as soon as I realised that our conversation was going to be a long one, I decided to take it on the extension in Leo's study; partly for privacy, and partly so as not to interrupt the half-fledged conversation which we had at last succeeded in bringing into being.

It was about Richard again. She was still worried. I had, of course, rung her up as promised as soon as I knew he was here, and that Sally was with him, but she was not satisfied, and I couldn't entirely blame her.

"There's something I don't understand, Clare," she was saying. "If it was one of his confidential assignments — a hush-hush job — I wouldn't be worrying. Well, I would, but I wouldn't be asking any questions, I'd be accepting it, as I always have, it's his job.

"But it's not that, it can't be. According to Sally, what he said was that it was just a social visit, to see Leonard again, find out how he was, and to help them in any way he could; enjoy a get-together after all the traumas.

"But it *isn't* that, Clare. I know it isn't. Why did he decide so suddenly, between the beginning of lunch and the end? By two o'clock he was packed up and gone, having cancelled a *very* important appointment! Sally heard him on the phone, and that's a thing he *never* does, letting his editor down at short notice. And then, why so insistent that Sally mustn't accompany him if it was just a social visit? Normally, he loves having her with him on trips, whenever it's possible, and they know they can leave Barnaby with me whenever they like. He's perfectly happy on his own with me, and behaves a *lot* better, I may say.

173

"I don't know what to think, I really don't. My son is a very reserved man, Clare, as you may have noticed, he would never allow himself to show anything like fear or anxiety. But *I* can tell. I'm his mother, I *know*. When he becomes excessively calm and off-hand . . . that's how he was when he left yesterday. He knew for certain that he was going into danger, grave danger."

How right she was. I paused, at a loss for a reply. Daphne was a shrewd and intelligent woman, who would soon see through any soothing lies I tried to invent.

"Clare? Are you still there? What is it? For God's sake, *say* something! Why are you . . . ? It's something terrible, isn't it?"

This jerked me into speech at last.

"*No!*" I assured her. "Nothing terrible has happened at all. Leonard's plane is late, that's all, he isn't here yet. But Richard's fine, I assure you. He's absolutely OK — except for his leg, of course, but I suppose that's bound to take a bit of time. He never talks about it, so I don't know what sort of injury it was, but . . ."

"It wasn't an injury," Daphne's voice was harsh. "It's sciatica — it's been troubling him off and on for over a year, but he hates to talk about it. He's ashamed of it, it makes him feel old. If it *had* been an injury — a real injury, sustained in the course of duty, he'd be much less furtive about it. An honourable wound, you see . . . That's how he looks at things. Always has."

"Oh." Again I couldn't think what to say. This new bit of information was surprising, but nevertheless entirely in keeping with Richard's character as I knew it. I felt the time had come to bring the conversation to a close, and so, reiterating my promise to keep in touch, and to telephone as soon as there was any news, I ended by urging her not to worry. What a futile injunction! It infuriates me when people try it on me; all it means is that they can't think of anything in the least helpful or encouraging to say: and so, to make amends, I added, "And if there's anything I can do in the meantime . . ."

Rather to my dismay, there was. My words (as is commonly the case) had been more a polite form of bringing the conversation to an end than a serious offer to add anything further to my already complex burden of preoccupations. However . . .

Richard's heart. Did I remember her mentioning it once before? Well, yes, now she mentioned, I did, though I had more or less forgotten about it in the interval, so unlikely a person did he seem to have a heart problem, and so few signs had he shown of any such disability — but then he wouldn't, would he?

His heart, then. What was she asking me to do?

"His pills, Clare, his heart pills. He's left them behind; they're still on his table, and the trouble is he needs to take them regularly, especially if he's involved in any strenuous physical activity. Really, he should be leading a quieter life altogether; the doctor has warned him several times. There's heart trouble on both sides of the family, you see. But of course he won't take any notice of that sort of advice; he loves his work, and *nothing* will induce him to ease up in any way. I know that, I understand it completely, his father was the same, but *at least* he should take his pills. And Sally's no good, *she* won't remind him, she hates having to think about it, she likes to feel that her husband is infinitely strong, physically perfect in every way. And *he* likes her to think like that about him, and so between them . . . Look, Clare, I don't know if this is too much to ask, but if you *could* find out if he's got a supply with him? And if not, persuade him to get a prescription from a doctor there . . . ?"

Well, yes, in a way it *was* too much to ask. There would be Richard's pride to contend with, as well as the fact that it was none of my business, as he might trenchantly point out. I would have to be superhumanly tactful, and, at the moment, I could think of no acceptable way of broaching the subject with such a man. Then I thought of Daphne, alone and desperately worried

175

in her big empty house, and felt that I couldn't refuse at least to try.

Uneasily (though I hope the uneasiness didn't sound in my voice) I said I would do what I could; and then, at last, we *did* ring off. But not before I'd heard the faint click of an extension being put down in some other part of the house.

It was just a little disconcerting. Had someone been listening-in to the whole conversation? Edwin, of course, was the 'someone' I had in mind; but it occurred to me that even if he had been eavesdropping, it really didn't matter much. I could think of nothing we had said which could be news to him. For Daphne's sake, I had been extremely careful not to betray any of my suspicions, and certainly I had given no information as to what was going to happen next. Well, I didn't know, did I? It was in Edwin's brain, not mine, that the scenario for the coming nights and days was taking shape.

So, pushing the matter from my mind, I decided to take advantage of Jessica's kindly suggestion that we should use the telephone whenever we liked. I made a couple more calls: one to my temping organiser, telling her that I was still unsure of when I'd be home; and another to Jason, just to hear how he was getting on.

Just fine, apparently. Everything was OK, except that the milkman hadn't left any milk this morning, had I cancelled it, or something? We sorted that one out, and then chatted on for a bit, about this and that. Our recent contretemps over the boletus had evidently been quite forgotten, or forgiven, or both, and we had a pleasant, laughing conversation, as of old. I finally rang off feeling a lot better. At least everything was all right at home.

CHAPTER XXVII

I must have spent longer on the phone than I'd imagined, because by the time I got back to the dining-room the meal was over. Even the washing-up was done, the kitchen empty, everything tidied away.

Where *was* everybody? And above all, where was Edwin? Who was he with? What was he up to?

The house was strangely silent. No stir of movement, no clink of coffee cups, no voices raised in idle chatter. With growing unease, I made a brief survey of the downstairs rooms. Only in the drawing-room was there a light on — a tall standard lamp casting a soft orangey glow into shadows, and highlighting the empty sofa, the empty luxurious chairs, the plump cushions unpressed by any human form.

Upstairs, then. By now I noticed that I was moving cautiously, on tiptoe, an instinctive response to the surrounding silence. The old stairs creaked a little here and there as I trod, but that was all.

Our own room was in darkness, like the rest, and when I switched on the light I was momentarily dazzled by the sudden brilliance. I don't know what I'd expected to see — it was hardly likely that Edwin would be sitting in total darkness, meditating — though goodness knows he had plenty to meditate on. Nor did it seem likely that he had already gone to bed — it wasn't much after ten. I was about to retreat once more after a cursory glance round the apparently empty room, when my eye was caught by a kind of hump under the patchwork quilt on the bed. So he *had* gone to bed then, despite the earliness of the hour? The shock I felt was quite out of proportion to the occasion: why *shouldn't* a man go to bed early? Especially when, to my certain knowledge, he had been up and about for a substantial part of last night. Even murderers need their sleep. More than most of us, very likely.

I moved nearer, conscious of an extraordinary reluctance to investigate further; and it was only now, as the first shock subsided, that I realised that whatever this hump was, it couldn't be Edwin. It was far too small. It extended barely half-way down the bed.

He'd hidden something here, then? Buried something? For a moment, hysteria gripped me, and I almost rushed screaming from the room. Then, with an enormous effort of will, I controlled myself, leaned forward, and very gingerly lifted the quilt a few inches.

The shock, for one second, was even greater than the first one had been.

Barnaby. Eyes closed, quite motionless, and for that one terrible second I thought he was dead.

But no. It was all right. He was breathing, normally, peacefully, the breathing of any sleeping child. His cheeks were rosy with sleep, and at the slight disturbance I'd caused, he stirred a little but did not wake.

Weak with relief, I simply had to sit down. Slumped in the rocking chair, I slowly collected my wits, and realised just how foolish I'd been.

Of course! The most natural thing in the world. The evening for the grown-ups was obviously extending far beyond the bedtime of a four-year-old, and so they'd decided to bed him down temporarily until his parents were ready to take him back to their hotel.

All the same, why had they chosen *our* bed? Well, why not? He had to be somewhere. And anyway, it wasn't *our* bed in any real sense; it was Jessica's bed, which she'd kindly given up to us for the visit.

178

Still, she might have told me. I might easily have wakened the child, barging into the room, switching the light on, and maybe — if Edwin had been there — talking quite loudly.

Then I realised that telling me would have been a bit of a tiresome business, as I'd been on the phone throughout the time when the decision about the bedding-down of Barnaby must have been taking place.

Besides, Jessica had very likely consulted Edwin about it — after all it was his room as much as mine — and he'd certainly have said 'Yes'. Not because Edwin is by nature a Yes-sayer, far from it, but because, as well as being vaguely fond of Barnaby, he was very fond indeed of the child's unqualified admiration. Very ego-boosting is the admiration of a small child, unclouded as it is by any rational assessment of one's good or bad qualities. Admiration was something Edwin needed, as a starving man needs food. How he throve on praise and approval! How happy, how kindly he had become during that brief spell of worldwide fame. What a *nice* person my husband would have been if only he could have been famous all along without having to do anything in particular to earn it.

Calmer now, my idiotic panic having quite subsided, I prised myself out of the rocking chair and tiptoed back to the bed.

Barnaby was still sleeping, deeply, peacefully, and pulling the quilt a little more off his face, I noticed that he was still wearing his blue tee-shirt. Well, naturally, they wouldn't have brought his pyjamas with them for such an unpredictable visit. As he slept, one firm, brown little arm was cradled protectively round some toy or special treasure; and looking closer I recognised the worn wooden rim of a tennis racket, the tangle of broken strings making little criss-cross shadows on the pillow.

Useless to anyone else, to Barnaby the battered object was an exciting treasure, and something in Edwin must have recognised this. Casually, without thought but with unerring instinct, he had handed it over to the child, and had doubtless revelled in the ensuing squeals of joy and gratitude, especially if Sally had been

179

around to note admiringly how good he was with children — far better than the boy's own father.

Why was Edwin so good with small children? How was it that he, a liar, a criminal, a would-be murderer, had such an affinity for that most innocent section of the whole human race — the under-fives? Was it in spite of his criminal tendencies, or — it suddenly occurred to me — *because* of them? Did they recognise in him a fellow-spirit, a dweller still in that primitive Garden of Eden without the knowledge of good and evil?

Gently arranging the quilt to cover the child's arm but to leave his face free, I tiptoed from the room.

Out on the landing, I had to think again. The silence throughout the old house was unnerving, and even more so now that I knew Barnaby was here. Surely they wouldn't all have gone out together, to the pub or for a walk, leaving him alone in a strange house? Would they? It was just conceivable that Sally, loving mother though she was, might have countenanced a short absence in the airy confidence that *"of course it'll be all right!"*

But not Richard. Awkward though he might be in the handling of his small son, there was no doubt that he was a devoted father, and intensely protective. No way would he have allowed the risk to be taken.

Or did they assume that since I was still in the house, it was all right? But no one had said anything about it to me, or even checked that I knew the child was there.

Or had they — it suddenly occurred to me — left Edwin in charge? And he, finding himself alone and unsupervised, the whole house at his disposal, might have seen it as a heaven-sent opportunity for . . .

Well, for what? For the furtherance of some nefarious scheme, I had no doubt. This time, no scenario came into my mind of what he might be planning. The important thing was to find him. He must be somewhere.

180

Once again, the ancient staircase creaked beneath my cautious tread. Once again I did my rounds of the downstairs rooms, finishing with the drawing-room.

Here, I was brought up short. It was in darkness. Someone, since I had last looked in, had switched off the standard lamp.

Suddenly bold, I stepped inside.

"Who's there?" I demanded, quite loudly, and switched on the light at the door.

A stirring, a heaving, a commotion behind the sofa made itself evident, and a moment later there was Jessica, more dishevelled than I had ever seen her, rearing up behind the sofa back.

"Oh, it's *you* Clare!" she gasped, her voice shaking with relief. "I thought it was a burglar. A murderer. A rapist. I heard those footsteps tiptoeing around the house, Oh, I was so frightened! It *was* you, wasn't it? Why didn't you say?"

"Well, how could I? There didn't seem to be anyone to say anything to. I looked everywhere. I looked in here, but I didn't see you."

"No," she had the grace to look slightly shamefaced. "I must have been behind the sofa already. I heard the door open but I couldn't see anything from where I was, and so I thought . . ."

"That I was a burglar, murderer or rapist," I finished crisply. "And suppose I *had* been . . ."

I stopped. What point was there in accusing her of arrant cowardice in leaving Barnaby to be raped, murdered, etc., while she lurked behind a sofa? It hadn't happened. No harm had been done. And people don't choose to be cowardly.

"Well, anyway," I said, as she clambered back over the sofa and settled herself, panting in one of the chairs, "here I am now. Everything's all right. I'm surprised you didn't realise it was me. After all, you knew I was still here."

"I didn't, you know. I didn't know anything of the sort. I thought I was on my own. I thought you'd gone with them."

With which of them? Where?

181

Well, all of them. You know. The others. No, not Rhoda, she'd had to go to the Nuclear Waste Dumping Committee. No, they weren't dumping nuclear waste, though it did sound like that, didn't it? Silly, really, calling themselves that when actually they were *against* dumping it, as indeed was Jessica, but she just wasn't a committee person, if I knew what she meant. Rhoda *was* a committee person, and since it takes all sorts, especially in a village . . .

I tried not to sound too impatient.

"Which of them?" I interrupted again. "*Where* have they gone?"

"Where? Oh, you wouldn't believe it! They must be out of their tiny minds! Didn't they tell you? Well, it was like this. We'd finished dinner, you see, and everything seemed a bit flat — you know, with Leo still not being here after all our preparations, and everyone sort of hanging about — waiting for you to finish on the telephone, I suppose, and also for Edwin to come back. He'd vanished — surprise, surprise! — as soon as the washing-up was mentioned. Well that's men for you, isn't it . . . ?"

"But where've they *gone?*" I insisted, heading off this familiar detour. "You said they'd gone out somewhere. Richard and Sally, do you mean? Or Edwin too?"

"Yes, well, actually it was Edwin's idea. He came bursting in — we were in here by then — he came bursting in, looking all — Oh, I can't think of the right word for it! Kind of lit up, as if he was drunk, but he wasn't drunk — we didn't even open the Sauterne, did we, with Leo not being there. Pixillated! I think that's the word — a kind of unearthly excitement; he was absolutely gabbling about it being a marvellous night, you should just see the stars — that sort of thing. And then, 'Let's go for a swim!' he cried, 'Come on Sally, how about it? A midnight swim!' and he began kidding her that the water would be wonderful, still warm from the summer.

"Well, you know how Sally is. She was jumping about like a six-year-old. 'Oh *yes!*' she said, '*Let's!*' and they rushed around collecting towels and things. I told them they could take what they liked — *anything* so long as they left me out of it.

"And off they went. I don't think Richard was so enthusiastic, he'd been arguing quite a bit, but Sally was mad keen, and so in the end he went too."

Well, he would, wouldn't he?

"And you?" I asked, "Didn't you want . . . ?" but she shrugged her shoulders, and executed a dramatic shudder.

"*Me*! *Swim*? at this time of year? Honestly, Clare . . . ! And as to the water in the North Sea being 'Wonderful' in October — they've got another think coming! But I didn't interfere. Let them live and learn!"

And then she added, a little defensively: "Besides, *somebody* had to stay at home because of Barnaby. I didn't realise that you were still here, I thought you'd gone with the rest of them.

I tried not to appear flurried or anxious as I hurried into my coat, changed my shoes.

"It's something terrible, isn't it?" Daphne had said; and, God forgive me, I had assured her that it was not.

CHAPTER XXVIII

By now there was no moon, and I had expected to be stumbling along in total darkness, but I had forgotten that darkness outdoors is never total. Even in the wildest and most out-of-the way stretches of country, there is always something, somewhere, glimmering and beckoning. Always, too, from this or that small town even as far as twenty miles away, there is a spreading paleness before which the blackness of space retreats a little, fails to be total. The very atmosphere itself is impregnated through and through with random accumulations of light.

In England, anyway. I recalled Edwin's description of the total blackness of the desert sky, and its dazzle of stars, and I wondered if all this would actually have been true, if only it hadn't been all lies . . .

By the time I had crossed the road and could feel the dry marram grass coarse and prickly around my legs, my eyes had become totally adapted to the nightscape, and I could see the dark curve of the sandhills quite sharply silhouetted against the paler sky, and I began to hear the faint, uneasy murmur of the outgoing tide.

Yes, the tide was well on its way out. From the crest of the dune I looked down on what seemed an immense expanse of faintly gleaming sand, stretching away and away to the thin white scallops of foam which marked the edge of the sea.

And here, to my dark-adapted eyes, lights seemed to be switched on everywhere, dancing, streaking, flickering towards me across the water. Lights from that anonymous low building on the east headland; lights — a whole line of mini-lights from a slow, flattened sort of vessel creeping lizard-like along the horizon: a bright, intermittent floodlight, coming and going, from some far-off maritime signal station; and, nearer in, several small, lantern-like flickers close around our wreck — presumably warning lights to guide passing craft from this dark obstacle.

The wreck. Until this moment, I had been in doubt as to which way to turn along the beach, but now I was somehow no longer in doubt. Sally would have chosen, I felt sure, to return to the scene of the afternoon's adventure; would she, even, have persuaded her escorts to drag one of the boats once again down to the water, in order to re-experience under the stars this afternoon's excitements?

Would Richard have allowed it? Would the ononpodo fit in with Edwin's plans, whatever they were?

For Edwin was up to something, that was certain. But what? If he meant harm to Richard, then why invite *Sally* to come for a midnight swim? Looking back, I can't think why the answer didn't spring to my mind immediately, so obvious was it. I can only say that it didn't. I think, maybe, my mind was being stretched beyond its normal limits by the enormity of my fears and also, in some way, by the hugeness of the night sky, the unimaginable distances that curved above me, pretending to be known and familiar. For was not dear old Cassiopeia almost directly above me? The Great Bear, the Little Bear, and Perseus, all in their proper places, known since childhood; and Orion, too, well up in the southern sky after his long summer absence.

All there, long loved and long known, and yet in reality totally *un*known, infinitely alien, beyond the reach of human imagination.

Something like that. In a kind of dream, detached somehow, I was aware of being in a hurry, of my feet sinking into the loose sand as I tried to run; and of my eyes peering intently into the swinging darkness, here and gone, as the distant lights moved with me, step for step, across the moving water.

185

'Peering intently,' I say, but at this stage I didn't know at all what I was looking for; nor did I know how frightened I ought to be. After all, there were three of them; Edwin would hardly intend to murder Richard under Sally's very eyes; nor could he expect to find an opportunity to make love to Sally under Richard's. Not that I thought — or ever had thought — that this had ever been in the forefront of Edwin's mind. What Edwin loved above all else was admiration, and this was what he was getting from Sally in full measure already, without needing to hazard his prowess any further. And what she got from him was, I am sure, exactly the same: admiration. That two such basically self-regarding people would ever exert themselves to break out of this cosy little bubble of mutual admiration and launch themselves on the perilous and uncharted waters of an actual love affair seemed unlikely in the extreme.

I hurried on, scanning the dark landscape as best I could. What did I expect to find? What did I expect to see? The three of them cowering somewhere, an untidy black smudge on the dim expanse of beach? Making stilted conversation, perhaps, reluctantly deciding what to do next? Or maybe already disporting themselves in the dark shallows, shrieking as bathers do? Sally shrieking, anyway.

No shrieks. No dark figures breaking the white line of the foam. And the black smudge that I presently saw was smaller than I had envisaged, and way down towards the water's edge.

"Hullo, Clare! However did you know where to find us? How clever you are! Oh, it's so exciting! They're having a *race* — all the way to the wreck and back! See? — D'you see? You can just see their heads — that's Richard, he's the one a little way ahead; I know it's him because I've been watching the whole time. Look! Look! There he is, he's just getting into that lit-up bit of the sea where the end bit of the wreck kind of sticks out sideways . . . ! *Look* . . . !"

It was always difficult to get a straightforward account of

186

anything out of Sally. She was inclined to start every story in the middle, the exciting bit, and only under patient questioning would she bother her head about the more boring whys and wherefores of things.

And so, patient I was: and this, I gathered, was what had happened. Edwin's suggestion of a midnight swim had, of course, delighted her, and off they'd gone, in spite of Richard's being a bit of an old stick about it, currents and undertows and things, *you* know. Edwin, on the other hand had been *wonderful*, had explained about the tide being just right for this sort of thing, and that there wouldn't *be* any currents. "It was his idea to come to this bit of beach where we were this afternoon. 'It was the best place for bathing,' he said, 'and the water would still be quite warm after all the sun there's been this summer . . .' Gosh, though, he was wrong about *that*! It was *icy*, Clare, it was awful! I only put half a toe in, just about, I absolutely *shrieked*, I couldn't help it, I came rushing out! I thought they'd be giving up, too, but Oh no! 'Let's have a race!' Edwin called, 'Come on, Barlow! Round the wreck and back. It's not much more than a couple of hundred yards! Sally can be umpire. What about it? Are you up to it?' And so off they went. I started them off — 'One-two-three', and — well there they are. You can still see them — they're very nearly there!"

'Are you up to it?' Thus had Edwin challenged his companion, with Sally looking on. What did he *think* Richard would answer? At that moment, with sick certainty, I fitted together the loose bits of the jigsaw. Edwin, eavesdropping on my telephone conversation with Daphne, had learned of Richard's heart problem, and had learned too, that he was currently without his pills. Far from imagining (as Jessica had supposed) that the North Sea in October would 'still be quite warm', Edwin had known very well that it would be icy (as Sally had found it), and had calculated that if he could somehow induce Richard to bathe in it, a heart attack would very probably follow — a fatal one if no

187

one pulled him quickly out of the freezing water. And no one would. Edwin could easily be too far away when it happened. And so none of it would be Edwin's fault at all. He hadn't even asked Richard to come for the swim in the first place; he had only asked Sally, knowing full well that Richard, consumed by jealousy as he was, would not tolerate the two of them going on their own. He would insist on coming too — and *that* wasn't Edwin's fault either, now was it! And then, when Richard failed to have the required heart attack at the first impact of the cold water, Edwin had resorted to the reserve plan of making him stay in it for a very long time, to make him swim, and swim, until his heart, un-helped by the usual pills, would surely give out? And this, too, when it happened, wouldn't be Edwin's fault, now would it? He hadn't *made* Richard swim out to the wreck. He had merely light-heartedly challenged him to the feat, with Sally listening.

"See? . . . D'you see them, Clare? They're practically neck and neck, they're just rounding the . . . Richard's got the outside track, the harder one, so if he *does* win it'll be a glorious victory! Oh, he's a wonderful swimmer . . ."

"So is Edwin," I found myself retorting, rather to my own surprise. Strange how I can't bear anyone else to belittle him, no matter what sort of awful things I may be thinking myself. "He once won the inter-county . . ."

Sally was instantly apologetic. "Oh, *of course* he is!" she hastened to say. "I only meant — well they're marvellous, both of them. Aren't they?"

I didn't answer, and she turned and looked at me, a tiny bit uneasy just for a moment. "Don't you think so, Clare? That they're both marvellous swimmers?"

"Yes," I said; and what I was thinking was, Thank God, Edwin's failed again! *This* ploy isn't working, either. Richard is going to make it: his courage, his stamina, his determination will pull him through, heart problem or no heart problem. Good for him! It was becoming clear that he was a match for anything which Edwin might contrive . . .

188

It was time, was it not, for one of those dark heads to be reappearing, on the other side of the vessel from where we had last seen them? All around the wreck, the water was more or less lit up by those little warning lights, and we fell silent, straining our eyes towards the rippling, uneven brightness.

Perhaps the distance to be traversed athwart the wrecked stern was greater than it appeared from this distance? Perhaps their speed was beginning to flag, as well it might. Or perhaps each in his own mind was saving his strength for a final winning burst of speed as he neared the beach?

And so we waited. And waited.

It was I who was the first to say that we must *do* something. Get help? Alert somebody?

"Oh *no*!" Sally at first protested. "They'll be *furious*; it'll spoil the whole thing!" And then, a minute later. "NO. Oh please, Clare, Richard so longs to win, you don't understand . . . If anyone intervenes, he won't feel he's really won!"

Did he feel he had really won, in those last moments of his life? We will never know. We *did* interfere, of course we did; we tried to drag down one of those boats, but it was hopeless, the tide so low and hundreds of yards of empty sand lay before us. So I rushed back to the house to telephone, while Sally started, at last, to shout for help, there where she stood.

Too late, of course. The two bodies were washed up at dawn, coming in with the tide, and Accidental Death by Drowning was, of course, the verdict.

And why not? I, after all, was the only one who had glimpsed the murderous hatred in Richard's eyes that afternoon. I, likewise, was the only one who was privy to Edwin's dark and desperate intentions. As if I had seen it with my own eyes, I could picture the two men plunging into the black and icy sea, each with murder in his heart. Each had set out with the intention of drowning the other, well out of sight behind the great hulk of the wreck; and in the heaving, treacherous water, locked in their death-struggle, each had succeeded.

*

189

I recall very little of the hours that followed, though the bits I do remember are intensely vivid, like one of those lucid dreams. I remember it being morning, and Sally at my side sobbing, "I don't believe it! It can't be true, it can't!" And I remember trying to console her, and noticing as I did so that I myself felt nothing — nothing at all. Like stubbing your toe. — For a perceptible length of time — a second at least — it doesn't hurt at all; the pain hasn't had time to travel the whole length of the nerve from toe to brain. Something like that. The feeling is on its way, I know it is, but I haven't yet begun to feel it. And, of course, I don't know yet what the feeling will be.

As I think I have made clear, Edwin and I didn't have at all a happy marriage. But, on the other hand, I've noticed over and over again that the most grief-stricken widows tend to be the very ones who had the most miserable marriages. Why this should be, I do not know. Perhaps, all too soon, I shall find out.

Meantime, I can only think of the various things that have to be *done*. Like ringing Daphne, for instance.

Strangely, there was no answer. You would have thought that, worried as she was, she would have been more or less hanging on the phone. There floated into my mind some words she had used when describing her son's heart problem; 'He gets it from both sides of the family.' This could only mean that she, too, had such a problem. Might it not, in this time of stress and anxiety, have caught up with her at last? I found myself half-hoping that this might indeed be the case; then she need never hear the tragic news at all.

What else do I have to do?

Ring Jason, of course. It occurs to me that I know no more what he is going to feel when the fact sinks in than I know what I am going to feel.

But one thing I do know: I am not going to tell him the truth. Any more than Sally (if indeed she knows it) is going to tell the truth to Barnaby. Each of our sons is going to go through life in the comforting belief that his father died a hero's death trying to save a friend from drowning.

It will be a lie, of course, but what of it? For Edwin, at least, it seems appropriate that a huge, flamboyant lie should be his lasting memorial.